Selfie

Allayne L. Webster grew up in rural South Australia and now lives in Adelaide. Her books include *Sensitive*—an IBBY 2023 Outstanding Book for Young People with Disabilities—the CBCA notable novels *Paper Planes* and *A Cardboard Palace*, the Adelaide Festival Awards–shortlisted *The Centre of My Everything*, and *Our Little Secret* and *That Thing I Did*.

selfie

Allayne L. Webster

TEXT PUBLISHING MELBOURNE AUSTRALIA

The Text Publishing Company acknowledges the Traditional Owners of the country on which we work, the Wurundjeri People of the Kulin Nation, and pays respect to their Elders past and present.

textpublishing.com.au

The Text Publishing Company
Wurundjeri Country, Level 6, Royal Bank Chambers, 287 Collins Street, Melbourne Vic 3000 Australia

First published by The Text Publishing Company, 2023

Cover design by Andrea Oerter and Jessica Horrocks
Cover illustration and lettering by Andrea Oerter
Page design by Rachel Aitken
Typeset by J&M Typesetting

Printed and bound in Australia by Griffin Press, an accredited ISO/NZS 14001:2004 Environmental Management System printer.

ISBN: 9781922790194 (paperback)
ISBN: 9781922791276 (ebook)

A catalogue record for this book is available from the National Library of Australia.

For Andrea

CHAPTER ONE

#FirstTimes

Dene Walker picked me to be her best friend. She had the whole of Tonsley High's year eight to choose from—and she chose me.

Me.

Dene's real name is Nadene Charlise Walker. Of course, everyone knows that. They knew it before she arrived mid-year, knew it before she set foot in school. They likely knew it before astronomers discovered Mars.

Dene is Insta famous. Her mum's been blogging about her since before she was born. Dene Queens— that's what she calls her fans—were a thing before *she* was thing. They followed her when she was in the womb. No joke.

My stepmum, Michelle, thinks it is a joke—a bad one. She says it's incontrovertible evidence that the world's gone barking mad. (Michelle likes to use big words.) She says when people celebrate people for doing absolutely nothing there's something very wrong with our society. I'm like *Whatever, Ancient One*, and my brother Luke is like *Okay, Boomer*—which basically makes Michelle emit steam from her ears. But it's true. Boomers don't get stuff. It's a widely accepted fact.

Besides, Dene hasn't done nothing with her life! She's done a whole lot of *something*. Scroll through her Insta and it's obvious if you know what you're looking for—which my stepmum clearly doesn't.

If we're comparing apples, Michelle has 320 Insta followers—*all* her real-life friends. Dene's has 1.5 million, and the tally keeps going up every day. There are always people commenting, saying how amazing she looks and how they really relate to that thing she just posted, or how a place she went to is, like, their dream destination. (Michelle is lucky if she gets a spam notification.) It's so inspiring. Dene has a clothing endorsement deal *and* she gets free haircare products. If that's not *evidence* of something special, I don't know what is.

That's why I couldn't quite believe it when the girl herself sat down next to me during second lesson and looked at my Maths notebook closely before saying,

'Hey, Tully Sinclair. How's it going?'

Who makes that sort of effort to find out someone's name? Dene was famous *and* a nice person.

'Hey,' I said. 'Dene, right?'

I had to play it cool. Famous people like cool people. Hollywood, the natural habitat of famous/cool people, is all about acting just that. Not that I'm from Hollywood. I'm from Jasmine Lakes on the outskirts of Adelaide. It's a brand new housing development for 'the up and coming mover and shaker'—that's what the real estate agent said. It *could* be Hollywood, but the South Australian version.

Anyway, the thing is: famous people make friends with cool people because they're a good fit, *not* because they're shallow or snobby or anything. It's just easier to hang out with people who are more like them. Dad told me that. He calls me once a week from his accountancy firm in Sydney where he networks with golfers, tennis players and pro-basketballers. He manages sports-star hedge funds. I used to think that meant he did gardening for a living until Michelle explained and I was like, *Oh, my bad.* Luke says Dad and Michelle are going through a trial separation. I don't think that's true. I think they just live a modern lifestyle, even if Michelle *does* call Dad 'a self-centred narcissistic prat' on an almost weekly basis.

'Tully,' Dene whispered, her mouth so close to my ear I could feel the warmth of her breath. 'This class sucks so bad.'

If I said I liked algebra (which I do) she'd likely turn away. So I agreed:

'Uh-huh. Majorly.'

She smiled at me. And I know it's a cliché or whatever, but her smile lit up the room. Her teeth were so white they shone. (I made a mental note to ask if she got free dental.)

Up close, Dene Walker looked just like her photos—which says heaps about her authenticity. Everyone says Insta influencers photoshop themselves or use filters. Dene is living proof that they don't.

Dene has blue eyes, dark lashes, glossy brown shoulder-length hair, perfectly shaped eyebrows and tanned skin. Her lips, earlobes and button nose are all in perfect proportion. Her only imperfection (online she calls it this) is a small scar on her left cheek. A kid in a playground clopped her with a swing when she was four and she had to get two stitches. Her mum posted the ED photo, blood running down Dene's tear-streaked face. Dene often reposts it, and the last time she did, it got more than 300,000 hits.

I don't think of Dene's scar as an imperfection. I think it makes her even more beautiful.

'You have a pretty face, Tully,' Dene said, right when I was thinking the same thing about her. She reached out and tucked a strand of hair behind my ear. She did it so gently, so considered, that whatever I was going to say caught in my throat. I couldn't remember the last time someone did that—not Michelle, not Dad, and definitely not my mum.

It felt *amazing*.

'You should wear your hair up,' Dene added. 'It'd look hot.'

Glancing at Ms Berryman, who was busy scribbling equations on the whiteboard *and* not-so-discreetly trying to un-wedge her pleated skirt from her bum crack, Dene nudged me and asked, 'Do you want to hang out with me at lunchtime?'

'Yes!' Then I tried to sound more casual. 'I mean, sure, why not?'

I'd have to cancel with my friend, Kira. We were going to meet in the library to do our art assignment. But this was a bigger deal. Way bigger. Kira would understand. She followed Dene too. I couldn't wait to tell her!

Dene smiled and a flicker of amusement crossed her face. I wondered if that was a good thing.

'I've got a feeling about you, Tully.' She pushed another strand of hair away from my eyes. 'I know

I've just met you, and I hope you don't think this is weird, but I think we could be great friends. Maybe even *best* friends.' She shrugged and said, 'Mum says I have a gift. She says I can tell if people are good. I see people and I just get them.'

My cheeks felt hot. 'You *get* me?'

'Yeah, I think I do.'

She linked her arm through mine. Her skin felt warm and soft. I wondered if she could feel mine buzzing.

'I don't think it's weird at all,' I said.

Dene Walker got me.

Me! Tully Sinclair.

No one in my entire life had ever got me.

It seemed too good to be true.

CHAPTER TWO

#SheMessagedMe

That night Dene Walker messaged me. Actually DM'd. There on my phone was the name of a girl I'd been following online for, like, *forever*. I stared at it thinking maybe it was some kind of trick. Like I'd entered the Upside Down on *Stranger Things*, or been snorted up an alien's nostril or something. I even pinched my thigh to check I was still alive.

'Ouch!'

Michelle and Luke, who were sitting at the dinner table opposite me, looked up from their Chicken Tonight, startled. We didn't have the TV on and no one had spoken for the last five minutes. Michelle had been pushing vegetables around her plate. Luke had already vacuumed up most of his. (*Teenage boys*, Michelle always says. Like that's an explanation for him eating like a complete pig.)

'I've told you before, Tully. Not at mealtimes.' Michelle put her hand out for my phone. 'Give it to me.'

I closed the screen and shoved it under my bum. I picked up my fork, stabbed a massive lump of chicken and put it in my mouth. 'Sorry,' I mumbled.

Michelle sighed and went back to prodding a chunk of carrot.

Luke kicked me under the table. 'Are you right, weirdo?'

I kicked him back. 'Stop it.'

Michelle waved her fork. 'Don't antagonise each other.' She pointed at Luke. 'And don't call your sister a weirdo. There are so many other more interesting *creative* terms you could use.'

Luke rolled his eyes. I did too.

Michelle used to be a university lecturer. She specialised in the Law of Succession which is basically the rules about who gets what when you choke and become worm food. That's how she and Dad met. Michelle did his will. They dated for, like, six weeks, got married (and had to change the will *again*), and then not long after that Michelle slipped on her backside in the women's loos at work and shattered four vertebrae. Surgery caused complications and after that her career flushed down the proverbial toilet and now she works from home doing consultancy. She only does it when she feels up to it though. She hobbles everywhere, sometimes with a walking stick. Luke has to carry our groceries and I have to do our washing. It kind of sucks.

The accident didn't do anything to Michelle's brain though, which is riper than an apricot's bum. (Apricots have bums—just look at them.) Her vocabulary is the size of mainland Europe and she insists that Luke and I get with the program and talk like her. We've attempted to Brexit more times than the British parliament.

'Tully is a self-absorbed, self-centred dingleberry,' Luke declared, smiling smugly at me. He looked at Michelle. 'Happy?'

'Luke is an egotistical psychotic megalomaniac,' I snapped back.

Michelle laughed. 'Ah! Good work. Worthy of a Shakespearean insult.'

I shovelled a piece of chicken into my mouth, then another, and *another*, and felt for my phone. Dene's message was burning a hole in my skirt. I had to finish my dinner. *Fast.*

Michelle gave me the evil eye. 'Tully…'

I scraped my plate clean. 'Mmmm. Tasty!'

'I don't suppose that's your father messaging you,' she said.

Luke snorted and slid back in his chair. 'As if.'

I scowled. What did he know? Dad's busy and I totally get that. He has an important job. People rely on him.

After Mum left us (something I don't really want to talk about), Dad stayed home for a while. Then he met Michelle, and soon after that the job in Sydney came up and they agreed it was a good arrangement: Michelle would hold the fort and work from home and Dad would earn the big bucks. Dad said he didn't want to disrupt our schooling by moving us interstate.

Luke thinks it's all a massive excuse. He thinks Dad spends his time going to parties and living like a bachelor. He's *really* cranky at him. They hardly speak. (My brother has 'anger-management issues' according to the school counsellor—I know because I snuck a look at his year-eleven report.) Dad says I'm the forgiving one. He says I have a handle on the bigger picture. I think that's true. I mean, I do miss him, but it's not like he's never coming back.

He *will* come back.

I pushed my plate across the table, stood up and slipped my phone into my pocket. 'Can I be excused?'

Michelle nodded. 'Homework first okay?'

I smiled. 'Promise.'

I went to my room and closed the door. I jumped

onto my bed and opened Messenger, relieved to see the little dot icon showing Dene as still online. There was a message from Kira too, but I skipped straight to Dene's.

You soooooooooo saved me today, Tully. Being the new kid is super-stressful. Thanks heaps. You're a star.

I saved her?

I'm a star?

I texted back, feeling kind of tingly. My heart rose in my chest, all floaty and warm.

You're welcome

I deleted that. I sounded like Michelle talking to her clients on email. I sent this instead:

Totally no problem 😊

I watched my screen. Dene's response came fast:

Everyone thinks I'm hell confident but I'm not

I couldn't believe it. Dene Walker was telling *me* this?

Before I could write back, another message popped up:

You seem like someone I can trust

I didn't hesitate: I am

Dene: It's hard being me. People don't know how bad it can be

I didn't believe that for a second. Being Dene Walker must be easier than breathing. But I responded with: Can imagine

Dene: ♥♥♥ Popcorn fan?

Me: Um yeah!

That *was* the truth.

Dene: I'll ask mum if you can come for a sleepover

A sleepover! At Dene Walker's house? *Whaaaaaaat?*

Dene: Tomorrow

My heart plummeted. Tomorrow was Wednesday. There was no way Michelle would let me go to a sleepover on a school night.

Dene: We'll tell the Gestapo we have an assignment to do together, k?

My pulse quickened. I laughed at *Gestapo.*

Me: Awesome. k

Dene: k

Me: See ya tomorrow

I waited, but that was where it ended. No emoji, nothing.

I rolled onto my back and hugged my phone. Then I went full dying bug, wiggling my arms and legs in the air. I grabbed my pillow, pushed it down hard over my face and screamed into it.

I tossed the pillow aside, flipped onto my stomach, clicked open my screen and went to Dene's Insta.

I thought of Kira's message, but I needed to know if Dene had posted anything about her first day at Tonsley.

She had. The update came at 3.50 pm: Dene standing outside of the school, a crowd of kids behind her waiting for the bus. It was like she'd hurriedly taken the photo without anyone knowing. If they *did* know, they would've jumped into frame with rabbit ears, funny faces and crazy poses. (I've seen other photos where people do this to Dene.) Her expression was sullen and the text said: *First Day Blues. #dene-queens #walkwithmewalker #ncwalker #youngandfree #livingthedream*

My insides sank. Didn't Dene just say I'd saved her? Why was her post an unhappy one? I thought I'd made her feel better?

I scrolled through the comments. There were hundreds, which I really respected because her post had only been up a few hours.

@dunnydog So hot
@mummasbaby Gorgeous
@sam_holden54 Damn girl
@hotchilli99 Dope
@jessica_watmunski What hair colour is that?
@bert_ernie_street Hang in there
@honeybiscuit Got a boyfriend?

13

@darren_lyons101 Bummer

@opensesame Call me please. I luvvy duv luv u

How could Dene possibly feel bad with all these people saying nice stuff to her?

I suddenly heard Mum's voice in my head. *It's not always about you, Tully Sinclair!*

I couldn't help feeling like it was.

I tossed my phone aside and forgot all about Kira's message.

CHAPTER THREE

#HerHouseForReal

Michelle bought the we-have-an-assignment-to-do thing. Part of me felt bad about lying, but I got over that pretty quick when Dene's mum pulled up in our driveway in her shiny black Landcruiser—the *same* car I'd seen in all those Insta pics with a smiley emoji over the number plate. I half-expected for the door to open and a red carpet to unfurl, with rope barricades and a security guard wearing dark sunnies, but it was just Dene and her mum.

'Tully!' Mrs Walker said as I approached the car. She hung a tanned arm out the window. Her gold watch sparkled in the sun. The stereo pumped rap music. She shouted over the top of it, 'I've heard so much about you!'

I waved to Dene, but she wasn't really looking at me—she was on her phone.

The screen door snapped shut behind me and Michelle hobbled outside, her greying hair bunched in a tangled pony. She was wearing an oversized Peter Rabbit T-shirt that hung halfway to her knees and she had on zero make-up. I cringed. Here was Mrs Walker looking uber fashionista in her blingy jewellery, reflective sunnies, bright pink lipstick and Hilfiger tank top. I couldn't see what she had on her bottom half, but I guessed it was ripped jeans, maybe a miniskirt.

'Hey there!' Michelle said, hand shielding her eyes. 'Thanks for picking her up.'

Mrs Walker beamed a high-watt smile. 'What's up?'

Wow. Dene's mum even spoke cool! She was the *epitome* of cool.

She added airily, 'A treat to meet you, Tully's mum. Our girls our studious bunnies, huh?'

Michelle glanced at me. The look on her face was like, *Is she for real?* But she agreed with Mrs Walker in a tight voice, 'Yes, they are. I'm Tully's stepmum, actually.' She put out her hand. 'Michelle.'

Dene's mum shook it. 'Kaz.'

'Short for Karen?' Michelle asked.

There was an uncomfortable pause. Kaz didn't answer.

Michelle said, 'Well, thanks for having Tully. It's

very kind of you.'

'Oh, it's no drama.' Kaz looked at me. 'Climb in, honey. Toss your bag on the seat.'

I turned and hugged Michelle. 'See ya.'

She patted my shoulder and whispered in my ear, 'If you come home referring to yourself as a bunny, I'll kick your cute backside.'

I got in and put on my seatbelt. The seats were soft and smelled like the leather cleaner Michelle uses on our couch. I couldn't believe I was sitting in Dene Walker's car. *Her actual car.* My heart was pounding. I was glad the music was so loud and she wouldn't be able to hear my thudding chest.

Dene turned down the stereo. She twisted to look at me and with a double wink she said, 'Can't wait for us to work together!'

I grinned, but I didn't do anything else in case her mum saw in the rear-view mirror.

'Thanks for picking me up, Mrs Walker,' I said politely.

She laughed as she reversed out of the driveway. 'Mrs Walker is my mother! Call me Kaz!'

'This is a cool car, Kaz,' I said, trying out her name. I liked the way it felt on my tongue. She made me feel like a grown-up or something.

'It's a lease vehicle,' Dene said.

I didn't know what that meant, so I was glad when Kaz explained.

'We have an agreement with the dealer to promote their business,' she said.

I guess that meant they didn't own it.

'That reminds me,' Kaz said to Dene. 'Did you do your post?'

Dene sighed. 'Yes Mum. I know the drill, okaaaaaaaay!'

'Don't use that tone with me, missy,' Kaz said. But she said it in a jokey way. 'Oh, and I meant to tell you that some boxes arrived. I haven't opened them as yet, but I suspect it's that new shampoo we agreed to endorse.'

'K,' Dene said, back on her phone. 'Maybe me and Tully could try it out tonight?'

I covered my mouth to stifle a shriek. *Did that mean Dene would include me in a post?*

OMG. I imagined us side by side, our soapy hair a mass of bubbles, holding shampoo bottles and poking our tongues out at the camera. I'd print that photo, blow it up, frame it and hang it on my wall. I'd kiss it each day before leaving for school.

Kaz turned up the music. 'I love this song!' she squealed. The bass thumped and she rapped her hands on the steering wheel.

I checked my phone. I'd replied to Kira about our art project but she hadn't got back. I could see from the icon she'd seen my message, but she'd left me on read. Weird.

Kira would understand, surely?

I mean, after all, it *was* Dene Walker.

Dene's house wasn't what I expected—it was so much more! It was two-storey white brick with a massive U-shaped driveway lined by neatly clipped hedges and conifer trees. I counted eight black-framed windows. The front door was glossy red with a big brass knocker that reminded me of Michelle's Elizabeth Arden Red Door perfume. There was even a gold bell on a chain.

A fluffy white cat sat on the doormat, tapping its tail as if to say, *Where have you been?*

Kaz scooped it up. 'Mr Biggles,' she crooned, petting it as she put the key in the lock. 'My baby.'

Dene groaned. 'Ugh! She loves that stupid cat more than me.'

'At least *she* purrs,' Kaz said.

I followed them into a white-tiled foyer. There was a grand carpeted staircase with a polished-wood balustrade and I could see all the way through to the back of the house, to glass windows and a sparkling turquoise pool. It was like I'd stepped into the pages of *House and Garden*. In fact, come to think of it, I think their house *had* been featured in that magazine—I remember a post about it.

'Should I take off my shoes?' I asked. Michelle gets grumpy when she's just mopped the floor. Dene's looked so clean you could probably eat off it.

Kaz laughed. 'Don't worry about that, honey. The fairies take care of it.'

'She means our cleaners,' Dene said, reading my confused expression. She dumped her bag by the staircase. I did the same. 'I'll grab us a drink and we can go upstairs.'

Kaz wandered off into a nearby room. I followed Dene to the kitchen. It looked more like an art gallery with its modern lighting, shiny cupboards and stone benchtops. There was even a sculpture with water pouring into a bowl. I wondered if it was a promotion gift.

Dene opened the glass doors of a fridge packed with wine bottles. She grabbed two cans from the bottom shelf, opened them and handed one to me. 'Melon Fizz, okay?'

'Sure,' I said, taking it. 'My favourite.'

I'd never actually tried it. I took a sip. It was really good. I wondered how much it cost. Michelle is extra careful with our grocery bill. She's always comparing prices and looking for specials.

Dene nuked some popcorn. She tapped her nails on the bench, waiting, hopping from foot to foot. 'Why does it take so long?' she moaned. 'Can't they invent popcorn that cooks in like ten seconds?' She took her phone from her pocket, clicked it and flicked through her notifications. With a satisfied smile she said, 'Mum will be happy. Seventy-five per cent engagement on that last one.'

The microwave beeped. She grabbed the bag, tipped the popcorn into a bowl, and said, 'Time to chill. Follow me.'

We headed upstairs. I couldn't believe I was going to see Dene Walker's real-life bedroom. I was even going to sleep there! This couldn't be happening, could it?

Dene's bedroom door was surprisingly bare. Mine has posters of celebrities and pictures of friends stuck all over it. Artwork too. I love drawing and painting. And watching movies with Michelle. Dene's door had a small ceramic love heart pinned in the middle and that was it. My art teacher, Ms Brian, would call it *minimalist*.

Dene opened the door and stood aside. I walked in, half-holding my breath.

I immediately spied Dene's colourful patchwork

quilt and recognised it from her posts. Sometimes Dene puts products on her bed for pics, and other times she lies on her back with her hair fanned out and takes a selfie, dots of quilt colour breaking through. I walked over and touched it without really thinking about what I was doing. I couldn't believe I was seeing it up close and real.

'Thank god we're finally alone,' Dene said, closing the door. She strode over, kicked off her shoes, and sat cross-legged on her bed. I did the same. She put the popcorn bowl between us. 'Sorry about Mum. She can be a bit hectic.'

'That's okay. I think she's cool,' I said, deciding it was better to say something positive. Besides, it was true. Dene's mum *was* cool.

It was the right call. Dene smiled. She stuffed popcorn in her mouth and talked through it. 'So that was your stepmum before?'

'Yep. I call her the step-monster.'

Dene giggled. 'Love it. Where's your real mum?'

She asked it like that—straight up, no hesitation. For a moment I didn't know what to say.

'It's okay,' Dene said, patting my knee. 'You can tell me anything. I call this the *Chamber of Secrets*.' She spread her arms wide and looked around her room.

Her shelves were overflowing with every beauty

product imaginable. I noticed a worn copy of *The Hunger Games* on the bottom shelf next to a thick book with gold lettering that read *Fashion Compendium*. There was a chair in the corner covered with clothes, and her wardrobe doors were open, more clothes crammed inside and shoes spilling onto the floor. Her desk was buried under boxes and papers.

'Did you just move here?' I asked, looking at the boxes. Then I realised that was a dumb question. I'd seen her house in a magazine. She'd been here for ages. *Der!*

'I moved schools,' she said. 'There were some crazies at my old one.'

'Crazies?'

She rolled her eyes. 'Fans who got a bit full on.' She shoved the popcorn bowl at me. 'Go on. Eat.'

I grabbed a handful.

'You didn't answer my question,' she said. 'What's the deal with your mum?'

I gave her a care-factor shrug, even though I *did* care, and said, 'Mum's an artist. She left because we were holding her back.' It wasn't the whole truth, but it was some of it. I chewed a piece of popcorn but found it difficult to swallow.

Dene's eyebrows shot up. 'She told you that?'

'No. I figured it out.'

'Oh. Does she visit you?'

'No.'

'Ring you?'

I shook my head. 'She used to call every few days. Then it was once a week. But not since—' I couldn't finish. The words got stuck in my throat.

'Since what?' Dene wanted to know.

'Something happened. She found out something bad.' I gulped. It was all I could do to not start crying. Explaining what happened to Mum not long after she and Dad separated was just too hard. 'Anyway... enough about her. Boring!'

'Well that sucks!' Dene said. Then she laughed. 'But hey, my dad's the same. He's a plastic surgeon and he's kind of career obsessed, if you know what I mean. I never see him.'

I smiled, relieved. 'I *do* know what you mean.'

Dene rocked on her bum, kind of jumpy. 'Yeah well, his loss. What does your dad do?'

'He manages hedge funds in Sydney.'

I was about to explain what that meant when she asked, 'So he doesn't live with you either?'

'No.'

'It's just you and your step-monster?'

'And my brother, Luke.'

She whistled. 'Right. Wish I had a brother. I'm an

only child.'

I knew that. Knew it from the times she'd written posts about feeling lonely. Knew it from the times she talked about her baby sister, Lilly, who died from SIDS when Dene was three. If it wasn't for Dene, I wouldn't know what SIDS (Sudden Infant Death Syndrome) was. She's done heaps of posts about it, raising money for charity so that doctors can research why some babies suddenly stop breathing. I thought it was a really admirable thing to do.

I waited for her to say something about Lilly, but she moved the popcorn bowl to her bedside table and flopped on her back, head on the pillow.

'Come here,' she said. 'Lie next to me.'

I did.

'Closer.'

I moved closer. Our heads were touching. Her hair smelled like fairy floss.

She pulled her phone from her pocket, switched to the camera and took a selfie. I didn't have time to pose or to think about what I looked like. She just took it.

She showed me.

There. On a screen. A photo of me and Dene Walker.

'You're really pretty, Tully,' she said, enlarging the photo.

I'd always thought of Dene as beautiful, never me. But when I looked at us side by side, for a second I saw what she saw.

I blushed. 'Thank you.'

She turned and kissed my forehead. 'I can't wait to tell you *everything*. We're going to stay up all night!'

My heart skipped and I grinned at her.

'I'll post that later,' she said, putting her phone down. It kept buzzing with notifications, but she ignored it and focused all her attention on me. She made me feel so special, so warm and happy. I couldn't remember feeling that good in a long, long time.

Dene never did post that photo. Or the ones that came after it.

CHAPTER FOUR

#SisterClub

Dene's bed was a trundle, so all we had to do was to pull out the base and put a mattress on top. After dinner (Uber Eats from an Italian restaurant) we brushed our teeth, put on pyjamas, and got into bed. Kaz told us to keep an eye on the time and not to forget we had school in the morning.

We lay facing each other. The window was open. The curtains swayed with a light breeze and moonlight streamed in. I could see the outline of Dene's face, her eyes bright and pretty.

We started talking and didn't stop. We talked practically *all* night. I don't even know what time it was when I finally closed my eyes.

I shared stuff with Dene I hadn't told anyone—not even Kira. At first I felt nervous like maybe I should try to impress her or something, but then I relaxed and completely forgot about who she was. She was just another girl from school. A nobody regular person like me.

I told Dene about how I want to be an artist. I want to live in a converted warehouse in New York, wear paint-spattered overalls, fling oils at giant canvasses and sculpt clay on a potter's wheel. I'd order noodles from the local Chinese, drink wine, and go to the cafe downstairs for coffee and bagels. I'd build stage sets too, for theatre productions on Broadway. Dene asked, *Why New York?* and I told her I'd seen it in a movie and it looked really bustling and exciting. Dene asked if I liked art because my mum is an artist. I told her *No way*, it wasn't because of Mum. But right after I told her that I wondered if it was the reason. Mum *was* pretty successful. Heaps of people bought her art, including TV actors and politicians. Maybe I *did* want to be like her? Dene made me think about my choices. She asked me questions no one else had.

Dene wanted to know my worst secret and my best secret. I told her my worst secret was the time my Uncle Dwayne, my mum's brother, made fun of me and whispered in my ear that I was fat and ugly. I tried to tell Mum, but she was busy with her friends. Dene said that my uncle was a crusty old sleazebag. I laughed at that. It made me feel better. I told her my best secret was the time Toby Hartley, who lived next door to us for three years, gave me a Valentine's Day card with a teddy bear on it. I was eight and I kept it under my pillow and kissed it goodnight all year. Dene said that was sweet and romantic, and that maybe one day Toby and I would find each other. I hoped so.

Dene's best secret was the time she brought home a puppy. She made it a shoebox bed and hid it in her wardrobe and sneaked it pieces of cheese, Oreos, and ham. Then her mum heard the puppy whining and Dene got into massive trouble. The puppy peed in the cupboard. I asked if she'd posted *that* story because I couldn't remember it, and she said she didn't because she actually stole the puppy from the neighbour's backyard. I couldn't help but laugh. She was only seven. Maybe she didn't know any better. But Dene told me she *did* know better and she chose to do it anyway.

The fact that she admitted it surprised me. And it made me like her even more.

Dene said her worst secret was the time a guy followed her online, sending her private messages and photos and stuff. She said it started out exciting because he was older than her and it felt special, but then he kept asking for them to meet up and she got a bit freaked and blocked him, and he then found her on Snapchat and she had to block him there too. Eventually he went away. She said she never told her mum because she felt like she was the one who started it. I told her it was probably my Uncle Dwayne. We both laughed hard. Then I was serious and I told her that she did the right thing and that she was really brave.

She squeezed my hand and thanked me for understanding.

Sharing stuff with Dene—*personal stuff*—made me feel good inside. I'd never had a friend I could share secrets with, at least not the really private ones. I mean, Kira and I talk a lot, and until Dene came along she'd been my best friend, but it didn't mean we shared everything. We have a lot of fun, *especially* doing art because Kira's a good artist too, but we don't talk about the things I hold tight inside.

With Dene it was different. Stuff spilled out. I felt free.

The next day at school Mr Khan separated Dene and me during History and Social Sciences after telling us off for talking for, like, the fourth time. Dene had to sit by the window. I had to sit near Mr Khan's desk. When I turned and snuck a peek at Dene, she made a love-heart symbol with her fingers and blew me a kiss. A boy called Harrison saw us, and he lolled his tongue and hugged himself, pretending to get all smoochie. Dene and I giggled, and Mr Khan threw up his hands, went and sat at his desk and banged his head on the table. I think that was a bit of an overreaction, but Mr Khan *is* a drama king.

After class, while I was at my locker Kira tapped me on the shoulder.

'Hey, you!' I said, smiling at her. 'Where have you been? How come you didn't message me back?'

'How come *you* didn't show up?' Her face was blotchy pink and her red hair looked like it might burst into flames. 'You know it's not fair if I do all the work, right?'

I stuttered, 'I, I can still help you to—'

Hands on her hips, she asked, 'When? Art is last lesson.'

She was right. I'd forgotten it was today.

'You ditched me to hang out with Insta Barbie.'

She looked at the classroom door. Dene was talking to Mr Khan. He was laughing at whatever she was saying and they looked kind of cosy. I wondered what it was about.

'I thought you had more brains,' Kira added.

Did I mention Kira can be blunt? I thought she'd

be excited for me.

'You don't know her, Kira.'

'Neither do you. You've talked to her for what, two days?'

I thought about what Dene had said. 'Some people just get each other.'

Kira rolled her eyes.

That's when I remembered Kira follows Dene's Insta too. 'You haven't said anything bad about her before,' I argued. 'You showed me that skirt you liked, the one Dene was wearing with the blue stars on it.'

'So?'

'So you like her.'

'I liked her *skirt*. There's a difference.'

'But you follow her,' I argued. 'I know you do. We've talked about how great she is before.'

Kira threw back her head and sighed. 'It doesn't mean I like her as a person. It just means I'm interested.'

Kira might follow people she didn't actually like, but *I* didn't do that.

I pulled out the books I needed. 'Well, I think you're being judgy,' I said, surprised at how comfortable I felt defending my new friend. Kira was probably jealous Dene had picked me and not her. 'And don't call her Insta Barbie. She's a real person.'

Kira raised an eyebrow. 'Whatever. Look, I'll tell Ms Brian that we did the art project together, okay? But next time you have to step up.'

I nodded, grateful to her for covering for me. 'Thanks.'

She half-grinned and I could tell she'd forgiven me. That's the best thing about Kira—she gets over stuff. She hardly ever holds a grudge.

She started to walk up the corridor, but she turned and said, 'Be careful, Tully. A snake that sheds its skin is still a snake.'

I stared after her. What did *that* mean?

I headed for class, desperately wanting for it to be over with. Dene had told me to meet her after school near the giant pine tree in the corner playground. She didn't tell me why, but I knew it was something exciting because her eyes sort of sparkled when she said it. I wondered if she was going to do a post, this time with me in it. I imagined a pic of us pulling fish-lips:

Meet Tully Sinclair, my best friend. This girl is the most awesome thing about my new school. I don't know how I lived without her. BFFs rule the school. #tullysinclair #bff #walkwithmewalker #ncwalker #denequeens #livingthedream

The day dragged. Ms Brian gave Kira and me a B+ for our art assignment. I owed Kira for that. We were supposed to do something on Climate Change and Kira had done a diorama of a stormy beach with little bottles washed up on shore and a dolphin tangled in a fishing net. It was quite impressive. She'd crocheted the net from kitchen twine and made the dolphin from papier-mâché. The water was scrunched blue cellophane and the clouds were deconstructed tampons—which I equal parts admired and laughed at. She'd even done a mini cardboard Donald Trump with his toupee-head buried in the sand, and a tiny sign that said: CAPITALISM SUCKS.

Ms Brian said that it was a well-thought-out piece, but she took off marks for the sand, which to be fair looked like dirt from Kira's garden. (Turns out it was. I saw an ant crawl out of it.) She also said that maybe the next time we use tampons we should cut off the string. I thought that was useful feedback, but Kira said Ms Brian had missed the point; it was a statement about how you can't just pull a string and make things better, you have to *work* at change. Ms Brian said the concept was too obscure. That's when Kira yanked out Donald and crushed him. Ms Brian walked away muttering, *Artists! Such temperamental creatures!* Which is kind of dumb because Ms Brian is an artist and it was like she was dissing herself.

After class, Kira asked me if I wanted to go celebrate our 'artistic independence' but I told her I had to go; Michelle had made a dental appointment. I felt bad for lying, but Kira had been weird about Dene and it was just easier if she didn't know. I said goodbye and headed to the pine tree.

When I got there, I was surprised to see another girl with Dene: Maddy Penrith from year nine. I didn't know her, but I knew of her. Everyone did.

Before Dene, Maddy Penrith had been the most popular girl at Tonsley High. She was very pretty, very blonde and very rich—very *everything*. She'd never talk to me. Kira once told me that Maddy's parents won Powerball, but I wasn't sure if that was true. I mean, they could've become rich from designing a successful app. Or maybe Maddy's grandfather patented those little plastic things on earbuds. (I learned about patenting from Michelle.) It could be anything. I wish Michelle bought Powerball tickets. Maybe then Dad could stop working so hard and come home.

'Hi, Tully,' Dene said, slipping her phone into her pocket.

I wondered if she'd just taken a photo with Maddy and I felt something inside me twinge. *Had I missed out?*

Dene said, 'You know Mads, don't you?'

I gave Maddy a friendly wave. 'Hi. You're in year nine, right?' Of course I knew that. I was more interested in how Dene knew Maddy, especially as she wasn't in our year level.

Maddy combed a hand through her blonde hair and said snottily, 'Hey, Sully.'

'Tully,' I corrected. But I had a feeling she knew my name.

'Right,' she said. The look on her face was care-factor zero. 'Soz.'

I shook it off and turned to Dene. 'What's up?'

'I have something for you.' She dug into her school-bag and pulled out a little white box tied with a pink ribbon. She handed it to me. She reached into her bag and pulled out another one for Maddy.

Maddy took hers, whipped off the ribbon, opened it and swooned, 'Oh Dene! It's gorgeous!' She plucked a little silver ring with a bluebird on it and held it up for me to admire.

I quickly opened mine. My heart leapt. I had one the same! I couldn't remember the last time I'd been given a gift when it wasn't my birthday or Christmas.

Dene stretched out her hand, wiggling her fingers. She had an identical ring on her finger.

'We're sisters now,' she said with a luminous smile.

'We're a sisters club!'

I put mine on my right-hand ring finger—same as Dene's. It fit perfectly. I stared down at it, my heart racing. *I'm in a club.*

'A jewellery company sent them to me,' Dene explained. 'It's not like I can wear three of them. Well I probably could, but it wouldn't look very good.'

Maddy hugged Dene. 'Thank you! I love it!'

I wondered how they'd become friends so quickly. Maybe they already knew each other outside of school. Maddy's parents were rich. Dene hung out with cool people. It made sense, I guess.

Dene got us to pose for a photo—just our hands in the shot with the matching rings. She took it and showed us.

'That's *so* cool,' Maddy breathed, grinning at the pic.

'Heaps,' I agreed. My face wasn't in the photo, but my hand was.

'I wish I'd got my nails done first,' Dene said.

'Well, I have to go,' Maddy said. 'Mum will lose it if I get home late.' She looked at me. 'See you soon, Tully.' Her voice was friendlier now, as if Dene had given her a secret instruction and she'd followed it. I was a *sister*, one of them.

I gave her a wave. 'Bye!'

As soon as she was gone I asked Dene, 'How do you know her?'

Dene zipped up her bag. 'We met at the bus stop a few days ago. She's really sweet, don't you think?'

'Yeah,' I said, feeling like I was swallowing sand. 'She's great.'

The truth was I was disappointed—*and* a bit annoyed. I thought it was only me that Dene was good friends with. I'd liked it that it was just us hanging out together. I wasn't sure I wanted Maddy joining in.

The more I thought about it, I realised Maddy wouldn't get to hang out with Dene in class. I would, and that meant I could be closer to her.

'Gotta go!' Dene said, kissing my cheek. 'See ya tomorrow!' She took off towards the carpark.

I looked at my ring, then at the pine tree. Dene had had her phone out just as I arrived.

I opened Insta and pulled up her account expecting the most recent post to be of her and Maddy, but it wasn't. It was just Dene. She must've taken a selfie before Maddy arrived.

She was leaning against the tree trunk looking miserable.

Sometimes you feel lost in the woods. #denewalker #schoolyardblues #walkwithmewalker #denequeens #livingthedream

A weird stinging sensation engulfed my chest. A few moments ago Dene had been happy. Did she really feel that way? Or did she feel the way she looked in her post? Maybe Dene *was* sad and she was hiding it from me and Maddy? She'd posted it, so it had to be the truth, right?

That night, Dene put up the photo of our blingy hands, tagging the jewellery company. She didn't tag me or Maddy and she didn't say anything about our sisters club. She said:

Putting sparkles in your day. #jewellerywizardsofoz #denewalker #schoolyardblues #walkwithmewalker #denequeens #livingthedream

I wrote: Good friends of yours? ;-)
She hearted my comment.

CHAPTER FIVE

#MissingInAction

The next day Dene wasn't at school. I checked my phone. Nothing. I checked all my socials, one after the other, cycling back to the first. She hadn't posted anything. I checked the icons that told me she'd been online—she hadn't.

I thought she practically lived on her phone.

I sent her a text during home group: Where r u? Then at recess: Collecting assignment sheets for u. Lunchtime: School's boring without u. Home time: Today sucked. Harrison got his crotch stuck in a foldaway chair and he had to go to sick bay and that was the best bit.

At dinner, I checked my phone whenever Michelle and Luke weren't looking. Michelle bought *the-pattern-on-the-fork-is-so-interesting* routine. I thought I'd be busted with that one.

Still no messages. It was doing my head in. What if something really horrible had happened to Dene? I had visions of her kidnapped by a crazed fan, tied up, swaddled in a blanket and stuffed into a car boot along with a shovel. I imagined an endorsement video gone wrong, a new shampoo causing an allergic reaction and Dene's face swelling up like a genetically modified beetroot. I pictured Kaz pranging the Landcruiser and she and Dene in plaster up to their eyeballs. I envisaged a surgeon frantically pumping Dene's chest—maybe even her dad—grabbing electric paddles and shouting, 'Clear! Hurry up, we're losing her!'

Michelle's voice drifted into my headspace. 'Earth to Tully. Hello? Anyone home?'

'Huh?'

'Ah!' Michelle said. 'There you are. I asked what homework you have to do tonight. I can check Daymap, of course, but it's easier to ask you.'

'Oh. Maths, I think.' But the truth was I didn't know what I had. I hadn't been paying attention. I was too busy thinking about Dene.

'Everything okay?' Michelle asked.

'Dene wasn't at school,' I said.

Luke moaned and rubbed his chest all lovey-dovey like. 'Dene, Dene, oh Deney-Dene-Dene!'

I pulled a face. 'Shut up!'

'I will if you stop talking about her,' Luke said. 'You're a boring track on replay.'

He'd overheard me telling Michelle about my sleepover and how much fun it was (*and* how much homework we'd achieved—which actually wasn't much). That, and I'd also shown her the ring Dene had given me. Luke was just jealous he didn't get to have sleepovers during the week.

'Just because all your friends are scuzzballs,' I said. 'Some of us have *real* friends.'

Luke snorted. 'Dene's *soooooooooo* real! All those posts are a thousand per cent honest-as.'

'What would you know?' I said, super-annoyed. 'Why do you even follow her?'

He shrugged. 'I don't. But I had a look to see what everyone was so into. She's pretty, but there's not a whole lot of substance going on.'

Michelle looked at him. 'And what would constitute substance?'

Luke pushed aside his empty plate. 'I dunno. A political opinion maybe? An insightful observation about a band or a movie? Something about the environment? It's all about her. Her and her stupid clothes and beauty stuff.'

'It's *her* Insta!' I spat. 'It can be about whatever she wants it to be!'

'Of course it can. But it doesn't set a very good example for all the dumb ones who follow her,' Luke said.

'You're the dumb one!' I yelled.

'That's enough!' Michelle said, slapping the table. 'We don't speak to each other this way. We hold civilised discussions and we express our opinions with grace and dignity. We *debate*. When you resort to name-calling, you've lost the argument.'

I stood up. 'I'm going to my room.'

'Don't you want to resolve this?' Michelle asked.

I glared at Luke. 'No, I'm done.'

Michelle smiled forgivingly. 'I think it's nice that you're worried about your friend, Tully. You think about people other than yourself. Have you thought about calling her?'

'Huh?'

'Calling,' Michelle repeated. 'It's this thing we did in the Dark Ages. We picked up a phone, dialed a number, and *voila!* Our friend answered and we held a conversation.'

She was right. I could do that.

'A call is a very personalised form of communication,' Michelle waffled on. 'To hear the tone in someone's voice, the inflection of certain words, the musicality of—'

'Okay,' I said. 'Thanks for dinner, by the way. The lamb shanks were good. Yummy.'

'Shank you very much,' Michelle said.

Luke groaned.

Michelle batted her eyelids at him. 'Meaty joke, I thought. Plenty of substance.'

I went to my room and checked my phone. Still nothing from Dene. Would she be annoyed if I phoned her? I'd already sent her a message. She hadn't answered, so that meant she was unavailable, right? What if I was intruding? What if I upset her by pressuring her to talk when she didn't want to? What if she was talking to Maddy instead? What if they were talking about me? What if I'd done something wrong I didn't know about?

The what-ifs were going to make my head explode.

If I phoned Dene, she could always choose to not pick up. At least she would see there was a missed call from me and that meant I'd attempted to contact her in more ways than one—and *that* meant I was a good friend.

I called her, my heart thumping hard. Should I play it cool? Should I act like I just randomly wanted to talk about something fun? Should I make up an excuse about homework or tell her what she'd missed in class?

She picked up on the fourth ring. 'Hey, you,' she said. Her voice had a smile to it, but she sounded tired.

'Hi,' I said, not knowing what to say next. Why was this awkward? It was never like this when I talked to Kira. I just said what I needed to say.

'Sorry I haven't got back to you,' Dene said.

So she *had* seen my messages. I wanted to ask why she didn't just reply *I'll get back to you*, but instead I asked, 'Are you okay?'

She sighed. 'No. Not really. Food poisoning. Fun times.'

I felt terrible! I was stressing about whether or not she was angry with me, and she'd actually been sick, probably vomiting all day.

'I'm feeling a bit better now though,' Dene said. 'Mum gave me one of those icy-pole things that put your lights back in.' She meant electrolytes. 'Not sure if I'll be up to much for the next few days,' she said. 'The good news is I've lost a kilo. Who needs diets, huh?'

I laughed. 'You don't need to lose weight. You look great already.'

'Thanks,' she said. 'And thanks for checking on me. Sorry I haven't had the energy to message. I've been watching *Fashion Wars* on Netflix. Better than schoolwork any day. Wish I could have the sick without the sick, if you know what I mean?'

'Yeah. I wish I could catch a tiny bit so I don't have to go to school either.'

'Come over here. Happy to share.'

I laughed. 'Nah, I'm good. Do you know what did it to you?'

'Mum ordered takeaway and she left it on the kitchen bench before reheating it. It was probably that.'

'Oh. Did she get sick too?'

'Yep. Not bad, but bad enough.'

'Bummer.'

She gave a weak laugh. 'It depends on how you look at it. Well, I'll probably see you on Monday, hey?'

'Okay. I hope you feel better soon.'

'Thanks, Tully. You're so nice. I wish I had more friends like you. Where have you been all my life?'

I hung up, feeling happy with myself, *especially* over the last thing Dene said. She thought I was a good person. Points to Michelle. Maybe Boomers do know some stuff.

Then I looked at my wall calendar and my heart sank. It would be two days until I saw Dene again.

Two whole days.

They'd be the longest two days in history.

CHAPTER SIX

#TattooYou

'I have the most brilliant plan!' Dene announced to me at lunchtime on Thursday.

I was at her side and things were back to normal. It turned out she didn't have food poisoning, but some gastro bug. (I was lucky *I* didn't catch it.) The two days without her had turned into five—five days that were a miserable blur. If you asked me what happened during that time, I couldn't tell you—I spent that time counting down the endless hours, the minutes, the seconds before we could hang out together again.

We were sitting in the lunch room scoffing hot chips. Dene said she had to start with plain foods so her stomach didn't get upset. She'd eaten icy-poles and sugary jubes for five days straight, and now she was faint and had low energy and was *this close to eating a rhinoceros*. I offered her my apple juice, but she said it'd have her in the toilet again.

'What's your plan?' I asked.

'We're going to get a tattoo.'

My apple juice went up my nose. I choked and coughed. '*Say what?*'

'You and me. After school today. I'm going to make us fake IDs on the artroom photocopier,' Dene declared confidently. 'Laminate them too. I nicked Mum's licence for a template. And I have my make-up bag, so I'll do your face in the girls dunnies.' She looked me up and down. 'So you'll pass as eighteen.'

I wiped my nose with my sleeve, not quite believing what I was hearing. 'Tattoos of what?'

'Not sure. But we'll get matching ones on our collarbones where we can hide them. You could get my initials and I could get yours. Or we can get a secret symbol—something only we know the meaning of.'

I thought about it, excited she wanted to do such a thing, but terrified about what would happen if Michelle found out. Or the school. If Kira had asked me, I would've laughed. With Dene I was actually considering it.

'What about Maddy?' I said, realising Dene hadn't mentioned her.

She shrugged and looked disappointed. 'Mads wasn't into it.'

That meant if I *was* into it, Dene would like me better.

I thought of the expense. 'Don't tattoos cost a bomb? Luke said his mate Tyler got one and it was over a thousand dollars.'

Dene wrinkled her nose. 'That's the designer ones. No one's going to charge a thousand dollars for a tiny star, or whatever it is we decide on. Anyway, I've got money, I'll pay.'

I twisted my juice cap. 'What if we get caught?'

She reached for my hand, held it, and looked me in the eye. 'I've wanted to do this for ages, Tully. Now at last I've found the perfect person to do it with.' Her eyes glistened and I could tell she meant it. 'Please? For me?'

I wasn't sure how I could possibly say no. 'Okay,' I said.

She dropped my hand and patted it. 'Send your step-monster a message. Tell her you're going for a bubble tea after school. She'll let you go, right?'

I nodded. 'Think so.'

'Cool. Mum's at pilates for at least two hours. There's a tattoo studio on Main Street. I've already made the appointment. You're Alexia. I'm Bronwyn.'

'Huh?'

'I picked us adult-sounding names.'

'Oh.'

She put a chip in her mouth, chewed it and winked at me. 'This is going to be so much fun, Tully. We need to choose a design. What about butterflies?'

I spent the afternoon wondering if I'd made the right decision. I didn't pay attention to anything Mr Yang said in English . On his third attempt to get my attention, he said if blank stares were a course requirement I'd get an *A*.

Meanwhile Dene had Art. Dene texted me to say there was a relief teacher. Relief teachers are basically robots programmed to say, *Do whatever you were doing*, and then they kick back with their feet on the desk and their nose buried in something they pretend is work. Dene told the RT she had heaps of photocopying to do. Easy.

I texted Michelle. She was happy for me to go out after school seeing as I'd been so sad the other day. Her kindness made me feel pretty bad for lying. She said it reminded her of when she and her friends used to go to the corner deli and buy Sunnyboys and Wizz Fizz—which must've been, like, one hundred years ago, I swear.

Dene met me in the hallway after the bell. She whipped out her handiwork: two credit-card-sized IDs with our faces on them. She'd used the photo she'd taken of me the other night at her house. I looked exactly thirteen-almost-fourteen years old. I had no idea how she thought we'd get away with it.

'Good, huh?' She shoved them in her bag and pulled out her make-up kit. 'To the bathroom and beyond!'

In the girl's dunnies, Dene worked her magic. She layered on foundation, contoured my cheekbones with blush, caked my eyes in black kohl and gold eyeshadow and blue mascara. Then she applied bright red lipstick and told me to smack my lips together. She piled my hair in a bun and handed me some silver leaf earrings.

When I looked in the mirror I couldn't believe it. I definitely looked older. All those products and endorsements of Dene's had paid off. She could totally get a job as a make-up artist.

'Gorgeous,' Dene said, evaluating her work with her arms around me and her chin on my shoulder. I grinned at our reflection. Everything inside me tingled with anticipation.

She was right. *This was fun.*

Dene handed me some jeans and a T-shirt she'd packed that morning. I went to use a cubicle, but she tugged her school dress over her head and dropped it on the floor, standing there in her bra and undies, smiling at me as if to say I should do the same. How her body looked obviously didn't worry her. I *always* thought about how I looked when I was getting changed in front of other girls. What were they thinking about me? Was it good or bad?

I wanted her to think I was cool about it, so I held my breath and did it. I took off my dress.

She beamed at me. We really were sharing everything now!

'Your boobs are bigger than mine,' she said, looking at my chest. She twisted side-on and wiggled her bum. 'But check out the junk in this trunk.'

I laughed. I thought of the posts of her wearing a bikini. And all the comments that she looked incredible. I imagined what they'd say if she posted photos of us with our fresh tattoos. Would they say I looked incredible too?

We got dressed and stuffed our gear into bags and then Dene pulled out her phone and snapped a selfie of us.

'Are you going to put that on Insta?' I asked, not really thinking about what I was saying.

'Nah,' she said absently. 'You ready?'

'Ready.'

On the bus to the city we discussed what tattoo we

should get. Dene's eyes glowed with excitement and I felt dizzy and lightheaded like I was flying. I didn't know I could feel this good.

'What about a bluebird?' I suggested, pointing to my ring.

She shook her head. 'No. Mads has one of those. I want this to be about us.'

That made me feel even *more* special.

I thought about her followers, the Dene Queens. 'How about a crown?'

She squealed and threw her arms around me. 'Oh Tully! I love it! You're brilliant! That's the best idea ever! And it can be a broken crown. You'll have one piece and I'll have the other.'

'Like in *Mean Girls* when Cady throws crown pieces into the crowd?'

She waved her hand dismissively. 'I haven't seen that movie.'

'Why a broken crown then?'

She didn't answer.

She pushed the button for the bus to stop. 'We're here!'

Giggling, we stumbled off the bus and onto the footpath. The bus driver closed the doors, shaking his head.

We were directly outside the tattoo studio. Dene

grabbed my hand and dragged me around the corner into a laneway covered with graffiti. Rubbish spilled from a skip bin and a dead rat lay by its wheels. Dirty water pooled nearby.

'We need to draw it,' Dene said. 'We have to show our design to the artist.' She pulled a sketchpad and a Sharpie from her bag. 'You're good at art. Go on. Draw it.'

I leant the paper against the brick wall and quickly drew a cracked-in-half crown complete with jewels and sparkles.

Dene took it from me and breathed, 'Oh my god, Tully! It's perfect!' She tore off the page, carefully folded it and put it in her back pocket with the pen. 'Okay. We'll leave our bags here.'

I looked at the dank laneway. What if someone stole them? My laptop was inside.

'If they see our bags they'll know we're students,' Dene said. 'Here, I'll hide them.' She took mine and shoved them both behind the bin. Then she linked arms with me. 'Okay, let's do this.'

A bell above the door tinkled as we walked in. My heart was beating so fast I thought it would burst, and my palms were clammy and I felt a little bit sick. I looked around. There was a glass display cabinet filled with bottles of ink, a counter with an old till, an eftpos machine, and a half-open cardboard box containing jars of lotion. Magazines were stacked on a tattered orange chair. The walls were covered with black-and-white drawings of tattoo designs: dragons, tigers, half-naked people, serpents, koi fish, cars, castles, the Statue of Liberty, a boxing kangaroo.

I heard a whirring sound like a dentist's drill coming from a nearby room. A guy yelled out, 'Be right with you!'

Hearing his voice made my blood drain. I started shaking.

Dene must've noticed because she took my hand and whispered, 'You're eighteen, remember? You can do this.'

A tall, burly man dressed in a skull design tank top and ripped jeans came striding out to greet us. Tattoos covered both his arms. His hairy chest had tattoos too. Even his head, which was bald, had tattoos. He was wearing blue plastic gloves.

'Afternoon, ladies.' But as he got closer, something about his walk changed and his shoulders sagged. '*Girls*,' he said, peeling off his gloves.

'We have an appointment,' Dene said in a posh voice. She pulled a bunch of fifty-dollar notes from her pocket and slapped them on the counter.

I looked at them, stunned. When she said she had

money, I didn't realise she had *this* much money.

Tattoo Man smirked. 'ID?'

Dene handed him the cards.

He took one glance and passed them back. 'Nice try.'

'But—' Dene began.

He turned away. 'Get out of here. Stop wasting my time.'

I grabbed Dene's hand to pull her to the door, but she yanked it back and snatched the money from the counter.

'You have no idea who I am!' she yelled at him.

'According to your ID, you're Bronwyn,' Tattoo Man said calmly. 'Now run along. Go play with your dolls.'

Dene huffed and stalked out of the shop, ramming the door so hard I thought it might snap off its hinges.

I chased her up the street. 'Dene! Wait!'

When she stopped and turned to look at me, she was crying. I hadn't seen her cry other than in photos. For a moment I didn't know what to do.

'Why is it that the one thing I want to do, I can't?' She sobbed. 'It's my body! Mine! Can't I have something that's just for me?'

I thought of the Insta post of us with our matching tattoos I'd dreamt up that would show the world how close our friendship was. But that's not what she wanted. She wanted something the public *didn't* see, something that was just for her.

'Give me the Sharpie,' I said.

With a confused look, she took it from her back pocket and passed it to me.

'Give me your wrist.'

She held out her wrist. I drew a half crown on it and a half crown on mine.

She took out her phone and snapped a pic. Then she wiped her cheeks and smiled. 'Thank you. That's so cool.'

I shrugged. 'No biggie.'

She cupped my cheek and looked right into my eyes. 'You look too pretty to go home. Let's get our bags and go get that bubble tea.'

Her arm slung around me, we walked up the street together.

'That was fun,' I laughed. 'Even if it didn't go to plan.'

She giggled. 'You looked like you were going to throw up.'

'Did not.'

Dene poked my ribs. 'Did too. And how about that guy saying we should play with dolls?'

'I know! Where's my science kit?'

She rubbed the top of my head. 'Nerd.'

Later that night Dene uploaded the photo of half-crowns on our wrists.

Future tattoo. Watcha think? #denequeens #ncwalker #walkwithmewalker #tatsliving

There were countless comments, all of them celebrating her idea. Part of me was excited it was *my* idea, *my* drawing, *my* wrist in the photo, and another part of me—the one I didn't want to acknowledge—was super-angry. It was the second time she hadn't mentioned me.

CHAPTER SEVEN

#SinkOrSwim

On Friday I got in trouble for not handing in my English assignment. I didn't even know it was due. I couldn't remember Mr Yang setting a date.

He gave me an extension until the following Monday. 'It's not like you, Tully, and that's why I've allowed it,' he said. 'But I'm trusting you won't do it again.'

He didn't need to tell me twice. If Michelle found out there was no way she'd let me go out during the week. I didn't want to risk not saying *Yes* to Dene.

'I'll totally deliver, Mr Yang. It's in the bag,' I promised.

He raised an eyebrow. 'Just make sure it's in my inbox.'

I saluted him for extra reassurance. 'Bet.'

In History and Social Sciences, Dene and I were paired for an interview task. It was the biggest bludge ever. We got to sit through a double lesson asking each other questions about our beliefs, our likes and dislikes, recording the answers on our laptops. It was like we were talking for real. It didn't even feel like work.

Kira was paired with Harrison, and I could tell by the look on her face that she wasn't too stoked about that, but unfortunately he was the only partner left in the room. (I wondered if one of his *dislikes* was getting his crotch caught in a folding chair.) I felt Kira watching me. It made me feel uncomfortable—*and* guilty. I knew I hadn't talked to her much lately. I told myself I'd get back to it. Michelle always says, *There are only so many hours in the day*, and I was starting to understand what she meant. You can't be responsible for *everything*.

Among the stuff I learned about Dene, I found out she loves the colour red, hates the smell of hairspray, thinks seagulls are dodgy sneaky birds, and strongly dislikes coriander. I told her there's a Facebook page devoted to coriander haters. She said she was already a member. That made me laugh. She told me she believes God is a woman and there's a possibility that the earth is flat. She also said she secretly believes (but had never told anyone) that the Upside Down exists for real, but in another dimension, and that the Duffer brothers had been there and that's why they could portray it so convincingly. I thought that idea was a bit out there, but Dene said to prove her wrong. I couldn't come up with anything. She said other dimensions *do* exist because we wouldn't have the word *dimension* if they didn't. I figured that was a good point.

In the lunch room, I asked Dene what she was doing after school. Michelle had said I could go out for an hour and there was a new boutique on Main Street I thought Dene would love. I'd seen it online. They had opening specials *and* they were encouraging people to post about their shop. It was a perfect endorsement opportunity.

'Thanks, but I can't,' Dene mumbled, scoffing a sushi roll. 'It doesn't work that way. Companies approach me. I don't go to them.'

She had a bento box with hand-carved vegetable flowers, sesame-coated prawns, inside-out sushi. There were even chopsticks and hand wipes. I don't know how it didn't get upended in her bag. My sandwiches came out looking like they'd been steamrollered.

Dene wiped a thumb across her top lip. 'Also, I'm going to the pool with Mads after school.'

I tried not to flinch.

'We decided this morning,' she added.

I waited for her to ask if I'd like to come too, but she didn't. 'Which pool?' I said.

'I think it's called the Rec Centre. Something like that.'

I knew the one she meant. It wasn't far from the school. Definitely walking distance.

'What about your swim gear?' I asked.

She shrugged. 'We'll scoot past home and grab it.' She pushed the bento box at me. 'Here. Have some. I'm not a fan, but Mum's crazy about it. I think she has a thing for the chef.'

I didn't feel like eating. I was annoyed that Dene hadn't asked me to go to the pool. But I took a piece of sushi shaped like a fish—salmon on a bed of rice— and I dunked it in the dipping sauce and put the whole thing in my mouth. It tasted like heaven. How could she not like this? I'd kill to have lunches like this!

Dene pulled the box towards her, took a photo, and shoved it back. She sat there typing something. Then she stood up and put her phone in her pocket. 'Gotta go. Mum wants me to call her. You've got Science next, yeah?'

I nodded.

'I have Art. Apparently Ms Brian wants to know why I spent a whole lesson at the photocopier the other day.' She pulled an *Eek!* face and waved goodbye.

I called out, 'Do you want the box?'

'Nah! Just toss it!'

I looked at the dark brown box with its cute little compartments. It was too nice to throw out. Maybe I could wash it and pack my own lunch in it? Or use it as a paint palette?

'Contemplating overfishing and the wilful destruction of our marine environment?'

I looked up to see Kira.

'Woah, that looks good,' she said, sitting down and digging in. She snaffled a prawn and something yellow that was shaped like a pillow. 'I have no idea what this is, but it's amazing.' She licked her fingers. 'The perks of famous friends, huh?'

'Spose.'

I checked Dene's Insta. There was the bento box.

This stuff is the bomb. Delish. Go Benny's Bento! You guys are the best! Get on down there, peeps. #buylocal #whatdenequeenseat #ncwalker #walkwithmewalker

Kira grabbed another prawn. 'Did Dene lose her appetite or something?'

'She had to call her mum,' I said absently, thinking about what Dene had just said about not liking the sushi.

Kira used a wipe. 'Even the towelette thingamees smell good. Hey, what are you doing after school? Wanna hang out?'

'Can't. Stuff on. Sorry.'

Kira was bummed. 'For real?'

'Yeah. I got an extension on my English assignment. Mr Yang went full bananas. I'm charcoal if I don't submit.'

'Copy mine,' Kira offered. 'Change a few words. He won't know.'

'What if we get busted?' I shook my head.

She suddenly looked miserable. 'But I've hardly seen you, Tully. Did you get my message?'

I didn't know what she was talking about. I checked my phone and found it. She'd sent me a gif of a parrot headbanging to the *Frozen* theme song.

'Sorry. It must've got stacked. Ha! That's cute.'

'Stacked?'

'Buried.' I shrugged. 'You know. When you get a lot of messages and it gets lost in the pile.'

'Oh.'

'I'll pin you to the top,' I said, pressing buttons. 'There. Now it won't happen again.'

Kira looked relieved. 'So...when can we hang out?' she pressed.

'Soon.' I felt guilty for being vague, and I promised

myself I'd get around to making it up to her. 'I think I left the assignment sheet in my locker. I'd better go get it. See ya,' I said, getting up to leave.

She held up the bento box. 'You want this?'

'Nah, just toss it.'

I walked off, imagining what it was to be Dene and to dispose of things so easily.

At my locker, I rummaged around at the back and pulled out my gym bag. Inside were my swimmers and a towel, still there from our beach excursion a month ago. I took a whiff. Holy gumballs. Hopefully it was nothing a squirt of deodorant wouldn't fix.

During Science, I sent Michelle a text saying I was going to the boutique opening with Dene. She sent me back a smiley face. Then I worked out my plan. I was supposed to be doing a worksheet on alternative forms of electricity, but instead I doodled what I'd say to Dene.

Oh! You meant this rec centre? I thought you meant the other one. What a crazy coincidence! If I'd have known I would've told you I was going too. Hey, seeing as I'm here, I might as well hang out with you. That okay?

That would work, wouldn't it?

Part of me felt bad about crashing her party, but

I also felt angry. She should've asked me. I was her friend. It wasn't fair to leave me out.

After school I hung back for twenty minutes to give Dene and Maddy enough time to go home, grab their stuff and get to the pool. I got changed into my swimmers in the girls toilets, all the while thinking about the other day with Dene and how she'd done my make-up. We'd had so much fun. Why couldn't every day be like that?

I put my uniform back on over the top and went to leave, but I felt sand between my legs. *Gross!* I went into a cubicle and brushed it out, wondering if it was karma for what I was about to do next.

At the rec centre, I paid the entry fee, put my bag in the locker room, and headed to the pool.

There were three swimming areas: a two-lane lap pool, a shallow paddler pool for mums and babies and elderly people, and a big pool with a lifeguard tower and stadium seating. It was echo-y and there were heaps of people.

I stood for a minute, holding my towel to my face, checking out the crowd. Maddy and Dene were sitting on the edge of the pool just to the right of the lifeguard tower, dangling their feet in the water. Maddy's blonde hair was dry. Dene's was wet. Dene was laughing and pointing at some random boy at the far end of the pool.

I dropped my towel on a chair, scurried over and jumped in. If I swam past them, it would be like they saw me and not the other way around. I told myself it was okay, it was just a dip at a public pool. It wasn't like I needed an invitation to be here.

On my second lap, Maddy spotted me.

'Tully?' she called out.

I stood up, neck deep, water splashing my chin. 'Oh, hi Maddy,' I said in my most casual voice.

Maddy looked at Dene. Dene looked at Maddy. Dene said to me in this really *annoyed* voice, 'What are you doing here, Tully?'

I felt my cheeks flush. Everything I'd planned to say went spiralling down the drain.

I stuttered, 'You said to meet you here, didn't you?'

I didn't wait for an answer. I dunked my head underwater and after holding my breath for as long as I could, I resurfaced, smoothing back my hair.

'I said I was coming here with Mads,' Dene said flatly.

I splashed her and laughed it off. 'Oh. I must've got confused.'

Dene looked at Maddy *again* like she was trying to figure out what to say.

I made my way over to her and tried *apologetic* instead. 'I'm sorry. I can go if you like?'

'No, no,' Dene said quickly, glancing at Maddy. 'It's fine.' She slipped off the side of the pool and into the water. 'You're here now. It's just a mix-up. Don't worry about it.' She smiled at me then and sank herself under the water. She swam a length, turned and looked at Maddy, and called out, 'You don't mind if she stays, do you?'

Maddy slid gently into the pool, keeping her hair dry. 'Of course not.' But she glared at me as if she'd swallowed a mouthful of chlorine.

I dived down and did a handstand, kicking my feet in the air. When I resurfaced, Maddy was fully drenched. 'Oops!' I said, covering my mouth in mock surprise. 'Sorry.'

Maddy glowered at me.

I swam over to Dene. 'Hey, see that boy at the end of the pool? Cute huh?'

Dene giggled. 'Oh my god, I was just saying that!'

I looked back at Maddy. I'm sure if she could've drowned me right then and there, she would have. Part of me understood. I might have got what I wanted, but I didn't exactly like myself for it.

CHAPTER EIGHT

#SecretFears

I checked my phone as soon as I woke up on Sunday morning. No messages from Dene, but there *was* one from Dad.

You up, Button? Call me.

I sat up, pillows propped against my bedhead, and searched his number. I hoped I hadn't missed him. Dad was an early riser, up at the crack to jog along Sydney Harbour or to ride twenty kilometres on his bike. He says in his business appearances are important—you can't rep famous athletes and simultaneously have a deep and meaningful relationship with burgers and an armchair. I thought that was fair. I wondered if it was the same for artists. Could an artist look like a bank teller, or did you have to dye your hair purple, wear red specs and Doc Martens, and saunter around in flowing hemp dresses? I figured you have to. Everyone needs to be taken seriously.

'Button!'

'Hi, Dad.'

'How are you?'

'Oh, you know...'

Dad laughed. 'That's what I love about you, Button. Economical conversation.'

'Are you coming home soon?'

'Hope to,' Dad said, but he sounded unsure. 'I think it'll be a few weeks yet. I have a big deal going down. I have to be here.'

A lump grew in my throat. I swallowed it fast.

'Got a big fish on the line,' Dad said. 'A whopper. Have to reel him in.'

'It's okay. I understand.'

'You always do, Button. That's why I love you.' He paused, and then said, 'How's Michelle?'

'Still making us eat dictionaries for breakfast.'

Dad chuckled. 'And your brother?'

'Still a pain in the backside.'

Dad laughed. 'Good, good. Well, I should probably get going, but I just wanted to check on you given what day it is.'

I looked at my wall calendar. *Mum's birthday.*

After a lengthy pause, Dad asked, 'You okay, Button?'

'Uh-huh.' But that's all I could manage.

'If you need to talk about—'

'I have to go to the bathroom, Dad. I'm busting.'

'Right,' he said, clearing his throat. 'I'll let you go. Talk soon, hey?'

'Sure.'

'Love you.'

'Love you, too.'

I hung up and tossed my phone down the end of my bed. Why'd he have to call and remind me?

But that was stupid. I'd remember it on my own. I didn't need Dad's help.

I slunk back beneath my sheets, thinking of Mum, wondering where she was and what she was doing. Then I thought of my grandmother, Dad's mum, talking to Dad in the kitchen a few weeks after Mum left. Grandma had thought Luke and I were in the lounge room watching a movie, but we were really listening, our ears pressed to the kitchen door.

Grandma said to Dad, 'It's not right for a mother to leave her children.'

Dad groaned. 'Please drop it, Mum.'

'It's not natural,' Grandma said.

'That's such an antiquated thing to say,' Dad said.

'Tara always was flighty,' Grandma said about Mum. 'She's *never* had a grip on reality. Her head's stuck in the clouds. All that art stuff. All those creative types she hangs out with. Trust her not to be practical about her situation! A situation like hers *requires* practicality.'

'I'm aware of that,' Dad said.

'Then can't you force her to—?'

'I can't force her to do anything. We separated *first*, remember? We had problems *before* she found out.'

'But can't you get her to—?'

'Mum! It's her body, her choice. I have no say. And besides, she's been told there's not a lot of hope. You know that.'

'But she has to try! She's a mother for crying out loud!' Grandma boomed. 'I understand this is hard for her, but she should be leaning on her family while she gets help, not cutting them out. I can't believe she's stopped ringing and taking your calls. Atrocious behaviour! Selfish and thoughtless and—'

'Mum, that's enough now. You know it's far more complicated than that.'

Grandma didn't listen. 'Those poor children. I hope they have *our* genes. I hope they end up like us and not like their mother. God forbid!'

A cupboard door slammed. 'I said that's enough! Stop right there, Mum. I don't need to hear any more.'

'I'm just telling it like it is,' Grandma said huffily.

Since that day, I'd not been able to get what Grandma said out of my head.

What if I was like my mother? It had become my secret fear.

I turned and buried my head in my pillow, smudging away tears. My heart ached. I missed my dad. I wanted him to come home. Understanding his work situation was hard. He thought I was good at it, but he didn't know how hard it was.

I rolled on my back, closed my eyes and tried to think of something entirely different—something happy. But no matter how hard I tried, my head kept drifting back to all the things that hurt.

My phone rang.

I sat up and grabbed it, thinking it must be Dad again. The screen flashed Dene's name.

I answered quickly. 'Dene? Hi. What's up?'

'Tully. Hey. I was ringing you because—' She stopped. 'Hang on a sec. You sound…Are you okay?'

'It's nothing,' I said, not wanting to make a big deal out of it. 'Forget it.' My voice cracked.

'Doesn't sound like nothing. Want to tell me?' She spoke gently.

'It's my mum's birthday.'

'Oh.'

I sniffed. 'Yeah. *Oh.*'

'And?'

'Dad just rang.'

'Right. What did he say?'

That's when I poured my heart out to her. I told her how I felt, how much I missed my dad *and* my mum; how I didn't understand how either of them could leave. I told her how I wanted things to be back to how they were, when we were a proper family. That I liked Michelle a lot—I even loved her—but I missed how things used to be.

Dene listened, giving me small assurances along the way. She said I didn't have to be tough all the time. It was okay to let stuff out.

Her kindness felt good. No one made me feel the way she did. Talking to her felt as if I was being wrapped in a soft, downy blanket and rocked like a baby.

After a while I said, 'I'm so sorry Dene. You didn't ring me for this.'

'It's okay. I'm glad I *did* ring you.'

'What was it you wanted?'

She paused. 'Don't worry about it. It doesn't matter.'

'No, tell me.'

She hesitated, but then she said, 'Look, I was going to say something about the pool the other day.' When

I didn't answer, she added quickly, 'But it doesn't matter anymore. There are more important things— like what's going on for you.'

She was letting me off the hook. She knew as well as I did I'd crashed their swim date.

I don't know why I said what I said next. Maybe it was because I wanted just that little bit more of her—*more* of her attention. She made me feel so warm inside. I didn't like myself for it, but it's like I couldn't stop.

'My mum is ill,' I said.

She sounded shocked. 'Oh, Tully!'

Her reaction made me go further. 'That's why she left. She didn't want us to see it happen.'

'That's terrible!' Dene breathed. 'Oh my god. I'm *so* sorry. Is it okay to ask what's wrong with her?'

I felt my throat closing over. I couldn't answer her.

'It's okay, you don't have to tell me,' she said. But there was a note of disappointment in her voice. 'It's obviously heaps hard for you to talk about.'

'Yeah. It is.'

'I'll be here when you're ready,' Dene said.

'You won't tell anyone, will you?'

'Of course not,' Dene said. 'If you don't want me to, I won't. I swear.'

I could tell she meant it.

'Mum doesn't tell me much,' I said. 'I'm still trying to find stuff out.'

'Oh, sure, absolutely. I get it.' Her voice was compassionate and loving. 'You know, I think with everything you have going on you're amazing, Tully Sinclair. *Strong.* Maybe the strongest person I know.'

At that moment, it didn't matter that what I'd just told her was a lie. She was saying the things I desperately needed to hear. I was revealing more than I normally would, but what harm could it do? Still, though, I couldn't shake feeling exposed. I hated talking about this stuff.

'I'll see you at school tomorrow,' Dene said. 'I can't wait to give you a big hug.'

'Me too.'

'See you soon, my beautiful friend.'

She hung up.

I smiled and lay back on my pillow. I wasn't thinking about Mum anymore. I wasn't thinking about Dad. I wasn't even thinking about myself.

I was thinking about Dene.

And it felt better than anything.

CHAPTER NINE

#GirlCrush

Late Sunday afternoon I was at the kitchen table drawing a portrait of Dene. I was using pastels, mostly muted tones, and it was turning out better than I'd expected. I hoped Ms Brian would be impressed. This week she'd given us free choice to draw a portrait of anyone we liked, and there was *nothing* I loved more. I hated being told what to do.

Michelle stood by the kitchen bench, sipping her coffee. She eyed my picture, tipping her head sideways as if to get a better view.

Eventually she came over and sat down. 'You like her a lot, don't you?' she said.

Well *that* was a stupid comment. Of course I liked Dene.

'Being thirteen can be a tumultuous time,' Michelle said. She saw my confused expression and shook her head. 'What I mean is, your feelings can be intense and that can be confusing. The way you feel can change quite rapidly.' She took a mouthful of coffee. 'I remember what it was like.'

I doubted that, but I went along with it. 'You do?'

She nodded. 'My body was changing. I was experiencing things I hadn't felt before.'

I cringed. I hoped she wasn't going to talk about menstruation and masturbation and stuff like that. We'd been through all that in Health.

'What do you like about Dene?' Michelle asked.

I kept my eyes on my work. I was shading Dene's hair, the strands around her face. 'She's...I don't know how to describe it. *Alive.*'

Michelle sounded surprised. 'Alive?'

I shrugged. 'You know...*Into stuff.* She's into doing stuff and enjoying it. And she's great to talk to and she makes me laugh. She's a really nice friend.'

Michelle nodded. 'Have you seen much of Kira lately?'

I erased a couple of smudges and brushed the paper. 'A bit. Why?'

Michelle rubbed her mug handle with her thumb. 'I'm wondering.' She motioned at the picture and switched the conversation back to Dene. 'What else do you like about her?'

Now she *was* annoying me. I'd just told her what I liked. What did she want? For me to write an essay?

'What about her influencer status?' Michelle asked. 'Does it make you feel special to be friends with someone so well known?'

I shifted the paper to the left. 'I don't care about that. I mean, I used to, but I don't anymore.'

It was and wasn't the truth. Of course I cared about it. I admired Dene's online following. I admired her confidence and everything she'd achieved. And it *did* make me feel special to be friends with her. Who wouldn't feel that way? But I also felt special when she was nice to me and no one knew about it. Dene wasn't posting *that* online.

'She's a very pretty girl,' Michelle said, looking at my picture.

I smiled. 'Yeah. She is. She's beautiful on the inside too.'

Michelle hesitated. 'No. What I mean is...'

I looked at her. 'What?'

She took a deep breath. 'Do you like her in another way?'

I held her gaze, not knowing what she was talking about. Then something about the way she was looking at me made it sink in. '*Michelle!*'

'It's okay if you do,' she said hurriedly. 'You can

like girls. Or boys. Or both. You can like anyone you want.'

'Well, thanks for that! Good to know!'

Michelle blinked. 'Tully—'

'She's my friend!' I said firmly. 'My *best* friend.'

'Okay, okay,' Michelle said, cradling her mug to her chest. 'I just wanted you to know it's okay. You seem...I don't know...like you have a crush. I want you to know I'm here if you need someone to talk to. Like I said, it's a confusing age. A lot of changes.'

I pressed my pastel into the page so hard it snapped. *A crush? What was she talking about?*

'I shouldn't have said anything,' Michelle said.

'You've got that right!'

She started again, 'It's just that you—'

I put the pastel on the table very deliberately. 'Just what?'

Michelle sighed, 'I'm worried about you, Tully. You're always talking to Dene. It would seem you're always thinking about her too. And you're on your phone so much nowadays, and you—'

'I thought you said you remembered what it was like to be my age?'

She stared at me.

'I have friends! I didn't know that was a crime!'

'Tully, that's not what I was getting at.'

'Would you prefer I had no friends?' I said.

'Tully, just don't lose yourself in all this,' she replied.

Lose myself? Why would I lose myself? And why on earth would she think I had a crush on Dene?

'When you're so focused on someone else,' Michelle said, 'you can lose sight of who you are.'

I felt tears coming. I didn't want them to. And I didn't want to think about me. It was nice to think about someone else, to care for them, maybe even to love them. There was nothing wrong with that.

I packed up my pastels.

'Please think about what I said,' Michelle said.

'Which part?' I asked, wiping my nose.

'All of it.'

In my room, I stared at my portrait of Dene. It was a good likeness. Ms Brian will definitely be impressed. I wonder what Dene will say when she sees it. Will she throw her arms around me and tell me she loves it? Will she praise me for being so clever? Will she ask me if she can keep it? Take a photo and put it online?

I've been given some amazing gifts, but this one is the best by far. This portrait is by my adored friend, Tully Sinclair. The girl has so much talent! #portraitofalady #artheart #denequeens #ncwalker #walkwithmewalker

I thought about what Michelle had said, about me liking Dene another way.

I held up Dene's portrait and brought it close to my face. I leant in to kiss her, but my lips found her forehead instead.

I couldn't kiss her any other way.

I liked Dene as my friend. That much I knew.

CHAPTER TEN

#ArtWars

'What's this about?' Michelle asked me on Monday before I left for school. She pushed my cereal bowl out of the way and turned her laptop in my direction. 'Here. This.'

Daymap. An interim performance update. My marks were looking less than spectacular. If they were a colour, they'd be beige. Maybe even grey.

I brushed it off. 'Oh, they send that to everyone. Doesn't count.'

Michelle scrolled through the information. 'It says that you need to show improvement; that you're not working to your full potential, Tully. Sounds to me like it counts.'

'Yeah well,' I said casually, 'I do okay. You know that.' I stacked my books and put them in my bag. I pulled out my portrait of Dene and showed her. 'Ms

Brian is going to give me an A+ for this, for sure. And I've finished my English assignment too. I'm all up to date.'

Michelle looked at my portrait and her eyes softened. 'It's very good, Tully. You put a lot of effort into it, I can tell.'

I carefully placed the picture between the pages of my sketchbook. I couldn't wait for Dene to see it.

'Did you think about what I said?' Michelle asked.

'Uh-huh.' And that's *all* I said.

Michelle patted my arm. 'Just don't get too distracted, okay? Remember to focus on yourself. And your other subjects too.'

'I promise.'

She rubbed the small of her back. 'Do you think you could help with the dishes before you leave? I think I slept wrong. My bones hurt. Your brother is still in bed. Apparently he doesn't have to be at school until midday. Nice for some!'

I loaded the dishwasher without argument.

Michelle hobbled over and kissed the top of my head. 'Thank you, sweetheart. We look after each other, right? That's the deal.'

I gave her a pressed-lip smile.

On the bus on the way to school I checked my phone.

Three messages from Kira and two new Insta posts from Dene. I looked at Dene's. One was about a nail polish that dries in ten seconds (yeah right), and the other was of Dene at her kitchen table with a—

My heart literally stopped.

There, in front of Dene, was a giant blank canvas and an array of acrylic paints. Behind that there were at least fifty paint brushes crammed into a pottery jug, five half-filled water jars, paint pallets, newspaper, coloured pens, a wooden art easel and sketchpads. Dene was looking over her shoulder at the camera with a pensive expression. She had thick smudges of pink underneath her eyes like a warrior ready for battle.

Art assignment. Getting my art on. Creative genius? Watch this space. #artqueen #heartofarts #artassignment #lifeisablankcanvas #denequeens #walkwithmewalker #ncwalker

I felt something ugly brewing in my stomach.
Art was my thing!
I scrolled through the comments.

@brendanlim_photography Beautiful AND talented
@hugme U so hot
@dancepants Use Crimson. Best colour
@laylikealizard Could u b any more gorgeous

85

@burgerswithextracheese is there anything u can't do

@hopskipjump_cassandra Can you do a painting of yourself? PLEASE

@dillon_colbert11 Ring me yesterday

@doopdoopdeedoop Canvas *my* heart

@dumblooksforfree is that eyeshadow or lipstick

@smashanddash Follow me. I love you

@downtowngallery if you'd like to sell through our gallery, please DM us

That last message surprised me. I clicked on it. It was a legit real-life art gallery in Melbourne. I scrolled through their photos. There were heaps of commercial artists. *They wanted Dene's artwork?*

I yanked my bag onto the vacant seat next to me and pulled out my sketchbook. I flipped to my portrait of Dene and snapped a photo of it—hard to do with the bus in motion; it took a couple of shots to get it—and I ran the Clarendon filter over it so the colours popped. I wrote:

Art assignment. Friendship is inspirational. She's beautiful. #artassignment #denequeenfan #dene-queens #walkwithmewalker #ncwalker

I hit post and watched the little circle spin as it uploaded. When it was live, I tagged *@downtowngallery* in the comments. If they were interested in Dene, they'd be interested in a picture of her too. Maybe they'd be interested in my art.

I sat back and looked out the window. It was the first time I'd posted in ages. Dene follows her own hashtags, so chances were she'd seen my post already. So what if she had? I hadn't done anything wrong. I'd worked really hard on that picture *and* I'd said she was beautiful. If Dene could post about art, I could too. It's not like there's a rule book on who gets to post what.

My phone pinged a message.

Luke: Creepy

Me: ??

Luke: Doing pictures of her now?

Me: Get out of bed and help step-monster

Luke: Sucked in, Dish Pig

He was such a jerk!

Several hearts appeared on my notifications. One of them was Michelle, another was Kira. I felt a bit sick. But if Kira liked it, that had to be a positive thing. Maybe she thought my artwork was good.

Seeing Kira's 'like' made me remember her messages. I took a look. All three were about joining drama group. We'd talked about it ages ago and I said I was keen, but I'd forgotten about it. Kira had sent me a snapshot of a list on the drama-room door. There, in black texta in Kira's handwriting, was my name. Her last message said: Now we'll get to spend heaps of time together 😊

I closed the screen. I didn't want to do drama group anymore. For one thing, it was three nights a week. What if Dene asked me to do something with her? I wouldn't be able to say yes. Kira would be disappointed, but she'd get over it. And I'd make it up to her.

I had to figure out how to do that, but right now my head was elsewhere.

When I got to school, I'd missed home group. Mr Khan caught me in the corridor and was about to tell me off when I explained to him that I had to wash dishes for my disabled guardian. That shut him up mega quick. I didn't tell him that I'd been so preoccupied on the bus that I missed my stop and had to walk an extra block to get to school.

When I got to Art, I found Ms Brian gushing over Dene's work. We normally had separate classes, but today Ms Brian had joined the two groups together.

I couldn't believe it. Dene's canvas was bigger than she was. Kaz must've strapped it to the Landcruiser roof rack. Or they paid for a courier. The entire class was crowded around admiring Dene's work.

'What an extraordinary effort!' Ms Brian gasped, standing back to gain better perspective. 'Is that—?'

'Textured gouache,' Dene said proudly. She glanced at me. Her face was hard to read, but she didn't look happy. 'And here I used a lacquered filler.'

Dene's painting was a mishmash of thick swathes of bright colour in semi-rectangular shapes. *Abstract*, Ms Brian would call it. But it was clearly a portrait of a woman, one who looked a lot like Kaz.

Ms Brian stroked her chin. 'You know, it reminds me of Ben Quilty. Your work echoes his.'

'Who?' Dene asked blankly.

'He won the Archibald Prize,' I said. 'For his portrait of Margaret Olley.'

Ms Brian looked at me with astonishment. 'That's right, Tully! I'm impressed you know that!'

'Yeah, well, my mum's an artist,' I mumbled, not really thinking about it. 'Tara Sinclair.'

'Is that so?' Ms Brian said slowly, pulling a face like she'd never heard of her. She turned her attention back to Dene. 'I think we should display this in the front foyer administration area. Art like this should be shared and appreciated by everyone.'

A few kids had their phones out, taking pics. Ms Brian was too engrossed to notice, running her fingers over the textured paint. She used to make us deposit our phones in a basket as we walked into class until this kid, Johnno, got his phone mixed up with a girl, May's, and it was a big debacle when they saw each other's personal stuff. The parents got involved and Ms Brian ended up in big, big trouble. Since then she's let us have our phones but she's had a rule of no photos. I guess that rule went out the window today.

Eventually Ms Brian asked us to go back to our seats and to get out our homework. I was relieved to see that most of my classmates had done the same thing I had: a simple portrait in a sketchbook.

I looked around for Kira and my heart sank when I realised she wasn't there. I always looked forward to seeing her artwork. *Where was she?*

Dene pulled up a stool next to me. 'I saw your post,' she whispered.

I kept my eyes on my sketchbook. I hadn't opened it yet. Ms Brian was on the other side of the room looking at Zac Watson's drawing of a Holden ute. *How is it he thought a car qualified as a portrait?*

'Are you going to show me the real thing or not?' she asked. Not prepared to wait, she prised my sketchbook from my hands and flipped it open.

The page slid out. She held it up and inspected it. 'Wow,' was all she said. She put it down, pulled out her phone and checked something. 'Do you know how many Likes you've had on that?'

I shook my head. I hadn't looked since I'd been at my locker before class.

'Twenty-eight thousand,' she said.

She must've been joking. I pulled out my phone. She was right. I also had more than a thousand new followers.

'Proud of yourself?' There was a sting in her voice.

I looked at her then. Her eyes were fiery. The way she was looking at me made my stomach turn. 'Dene, I—'

'I had to change schools cos of people doing stuff like this.'

I didn't know what to say.

'I thought you were different, Tully.'

That hurt. 'I *am* different!'

She crossed her arms. 'Doesn't seem like it.'

I felt tears coming. I couldn't stop them. I peered around the room to see if anyone was watching us, but they were focused on Ms Brian who was making her way to our table.

'I worked really hard on that drawing,' I whispered. 'I did it for you. *My friend.*'

Now it was Dene's turn to not know what to say.

'I was going to show you before class,' I said, 'but I was running late and I—'

'So you posted it?'

'You posted *your* artwork!'

'So?' Dene hissed. 'Posting stuff is what I do!'

'Oh, so I'm not allowed to post mine?'

Her eyes narrowed. 'Kind of convenient you did a portrait of me. If you'd done one of your step-monster, do you think you'd get as many likes?'

She was right. I probably would've got five at the most.

'My followers follow *me*,' she spat. 'You posted a picture of me and now they're following you. Feel good, does it?'

'I didn't do it for followers!'

I hid the picture in my sketchbook and packed up my stuff. I had to get out of there. Tears were clouding my vision. None of this was turning out the way I'd hoped.

'Why did you do it?' Dene pressed.

Grabbing my things, I slid off my stool, turned my back and walked out. I heard Ms Brian call out to me, but all I said was 'stomach ache' and kept moving.

I went straight to the girls toilets, into a cubicle and locked the door. I put the toilet seat down, sat on it and cried.

I'd worked so hard on that drawing. All I wanted was for Dene to like it. Now she thought I'd done it to get followers. How could she think that? Yeah, I *may* have posted it because I was a bit jealous of her doing art when art was my thing, and I wanted that Melbourne art gallery to see my work too, but I *never* did it to get famous or anything!

I spun the toilet paper roll and ripped off a bunch. I barely heard the main door open. Someone was calling out to me.

Dene.

'Just leave me alone,' I said.

'Tully, come out here and talk to me.'

'Why?' I sobbed. 'So you can get mad at me again?'

'Tully, please…'

I wiped my face. I bet I looked all red and puffy.

'*Please?*' she called.

Shaking, I stood up and opened the door. Dene was standing right there in the doorway, crying too. *Why was she crying?*

'You don't understand,' she sniffed. 'I had a bad time at my last school. I thought…well, I thought…'

'You thought I was using you?'

She nodded and wiped her nose.

'I wouldn't do that.'

She looked at me a moment longer, then threw her arms around me and hugged me so tight I could barely breathe.

I hugged her back, relief washing through me. She didn't think I was a bad person anymore.

After what seemed like ages, she let go and stood back, laughing and crying at the same time. 'I'm so sorry, Tully. I overreacted.'

'It's okay,' I said, rubbing my wet cheeks. 'I shouldn't have posted it. I didn't think it through. I'll take it down...'

'Nah, it's okay,' she said. 'Just maybe don't do that kind of thing again. My mum gets real mad.'

I didn't like the idea of Kaz being angry with me. She might stop me from hanging out with Dene.

'Why does she get upset?' I asked.

Dene rolled her eyes. 'It's a business thing. She likes to control my image. Don't worry about it. I'll explain it to her and she'll understand.' She reached for my hand, took it and stroked my bluebird ring. 'It was a nice thing to do, Tully. And it's a really beautiful picture. I'm sorry I spoiled it by getting so angry.'

'It took me ages,' I said. 'I worked really hard.'

'It shows.' She dropped my hand to fiddle with her own ring.

'Your picture is good too,' I said. 'Ms Brian loves it.'

She shrugged. 'Nah. I fluked it.'

'No...' I insisted. 'It's *really* good. You're mega talented.'

'I had some help,' she mumbled, not looking at me. I wanted to ask what that meant, but she said, 'Come on, we should go back. Ms Brian needs to see your picture. She'll give you an A for sure.'

'You think?' I said, hopeful.

Dene smiled. 'Definitely.'

But Ms Brian gave me a B.

She gave Dene an A+.

And even though we'd argued and worked it out and I was grateful for that, I was still upset. I wondered if Dene was still angry with me too.

Later, I messaged Kira to ask why she wasn't in class.

She left me on read.

CHAPTER ELEVEN

#DandelionWishes

'Coops is in town,' Dene announced one Friday after school. We were lying on our backs on the edge of the school oval in the shade of a gum tree. I was midway through scoffing a finger bun that I hadn't got around to eating at lunchtime. The butter was thick, the way I liked it, and it oozed out the sides.

'Who's Coops?' I asked, licking icing from my thumb.

Dene leant over me and came at my finger bun from the other end, taking a huge bite.

I batted her away. 'Hey! Get your own!'

She munched it quick and took *another* bite. Now our noses were touching. We giggled, cheeks bulging, coconut bits flying from our lips.

Dene coughed and rolled onto her back. Butter was smudged up her cheek. I pretended to lick it off and she shoved me away, cackling hard. We wrestled like little kids in a sandpit, rolling from side to side. We mucked around some more before Dene grabbed me in a headlock, pulled out her phone, held it at length and took a photo of us. She looked at it, grinning, then closed the screen.

'Who's in town?' I asked.

'My boyfriend, Coops. Short for Cooper.'

'*Boyfriend?*'

I didn't know Dene had a boyfriend. She'd never mentioned him, never posted anything. I don't know why, but I felt kind of left out—I'd been missing a crucial bit of information.

Dene picked a blade of grass and ran it between her fingers. 'His mum is a friend of my mum's. They live in Kalgoorlie. They're here visiting Coops' granddad who's in a nursing home.'

I rolled onto my stomach, propped on my elbows. 'Got a pic?'

She found one and showed me. 'Cute huh?'

I looked at the boy in the picture. He was tall with spiked brown hair and dimples. *Very* good looking.

'How old is he?' I asked.

'Fourteen.'

'Have you—?' I pulled kissy lips.

She gave me a devious smile. 'Of course!'

I'd never had a boyfriend. I wasn't even thinking about trying to get one. Occasionally I'd see a cute boy in a movie Michelle and I were watching, and she'd nudge me in the ribs and we'd laugh, but that was it. The boys in my year irritated me more than anything. Most of the time I wished they weren't there.

'Is he a good kisser?' I asked.

She had a dreamy look in her eyes. 'Definitely.'

I totally believed her. Of course she'd kissed a boy! She was Dene Walker.

'Do you want to meet him?' she asked.

I couldn't believe it. '*Really?*'

She nodded. 'He's coming over with his dad for dinner tonight. Do you want to come for a swim?'

'I'll ask Michelle.'

I fired off a text. She came back straightaway with a smiley face. I showed Dene.

'Yay!' She went to hug me, but she stopped. 'Oh my god! Look!' She reached out for something just past my head—a dandelion. She carefully plucked it from the grass and held it up to me. 'Make a wish,' she said.

I didn't need to think about it too long. I closed my eyes and blew.

She smiled. 'What'd you wish for?'

'I'm not telling! It won't come true.'

She tickled me. 'Go on, tell me!'

I shrieked, rolling around, my dress hiking up, my stomach cramping with laughter. I grabbed her hands, my legs tangled with hers, kicking half-heartedly, twisting and pulling. Gasping, we finally stopped.

She looked at me with the most radiant smile. 'You're the absolute best, Tully Sinclair.'

I squished her nose with the tip of my finger. 'Same.'

I'd wished upon that dandelion that we'd be friends forever.

If I kept it a secret, maybe it would come true.

On the way to Dene's house, I realised when I'd made that wish, I didn't even stop to think of the bad stuff in my life. I didn't wish to change any of it.

Dene was all I needed.

Coops turned out to be annoying friendly. Annoying, because I wanted to hate him.

Dene couldn't stop staring at him. Since we'd arrived at her place, she'd barely looked my way. She followed him around like a puppy dog, trailing after him everywhere he went. Her tongue was almost hanging out of her head.

'Dene said you're a really good artist,' Coops said to me, as the three of us sat on the edge of the pool with our feet in the water. Dene was on the other side of him, their arms touching. He wore black board shorts, a couple of leather bracelets and a shark tooth necklace. Beads of water ran down his bare chest.

'Yeah, I like drawing,' I agreed, wondering what else Dene had said.

'Could you draw me?' Coops asked.

'She could draw *anyone*,' Dene volunteered eagerly. 'She's so talented.'

That made me feel happy. She was obviously proud of me.

'I don't know if I'm *that* good,' I said, trying not to sound up myself.

'Don't listen to her,' Dene said. 'She's just being modest.'

'Dene!' Kaz interrupted. 'Did you put on sunscreen?'

Kaz was sprawled on a sunlounge under an umbrella on the other side of the pool, drinking champagne cocktails with Cooper's dad, who looked like an older version of Cooper. He kept getting up to fill Kaz's glass, fussing over her, adjusting the umbrella, offering her snacks. Kaz looked like a model with her long bronzed legs, her red-and-white striped bikini and her reflective sunnies. Even her hair was perfectly styled.

'Yes, I put on sunscreen!' Dene yelled. She quietly snickered to us, 'Bet she hasn't. Have a look at her legs. Talk about baked.'

'I dunno,' Coops said with a cheeky grin. 'Your mum looks all right to me.'

Gross!

Dene swatted him. *'Ew!'*

He scooped a handful of water and flicked it at her. She pushed him and his shoulder knocked into mine. I shuffled over, putting a gap between us.

'Wanna go to the movies tomorrow?' I asked, leaning forward to look at Dene.

Coops clapped his hands. 'I'm in. What are we seeing?'

Great. I didn't invite him!

'I was thinking we could see that new one about tornados,' I said. 'It's my birthday, so Michelle will let me go.'

Dene looked at me, surprised. 'It's your birthday?'

My cheeks burned. Why did she have to say that in front of Coops?

I laughed it off. 'You know that. I told you.'

But the truth was I probably didn't tell her. I assumed she would've seen it on one of my profiles; that she would've gone looking for it. That's what friends do—they know that stuff. I knew hers: 23 December. Kaz referred to Dene as her *Christmas miracle.* Dene had complained about how much it sucks to have your birthday close to Christmas. Everyone forgets you.

As if *anyone* would ever forget Dene.

Dene kicked the water and said, 'Oh, I remember now.'

I knew she was lying.

'Can you come?' I pressed.

'Sure.' But that's all she said. Then she cried out, 'Last one in is a rotten egg!' and jumped into the pool.

Coops dived in after her. So did I. Kaz cranked up the music. She raised her glass as if to say, *Have fun, kids!*

Coops and Dene mucked around, shouting and splashing each other. I tried to join in, but they didn't really want me. After a while it was as if I wasn't there. I was like a spare pool floaty, bobbing around. I wondered why Dene had invited me.

I swam over to a giant inflatable thong and clung to it, watching them. I laughed at their antics, but I didn't mean it; I did it to make it look like I was having a good time. But I was glad Coops lived interstate and was only staying for a few days. The sooner he was gone, the better.

'Dene!' Kaz called, holding up Dene's phone. 'It's ringing!'

Dene swam over to the ladder and climbed out. She

grabbed a towel and patted herself dry, then she took the phone from her mum.

'It's Mads,' she said. 'I need to pee. I'll ring her back after I go to the bathroom.' She walked off into the house.

Did Dene *really* need to go to the loo? Or didn't she want anyone to listen? What did she have to discuss with Maddy that was so private?

Kaz went back to her cocktail and getting Coops's dad to rub cream on her back. They looked pretty cosy. I wondered if there was something a bit weird about Dene liking Coops and her mum liking his dad. I'd google it later to check if that was an okay thing.

Coops swam over to me. 'Hey,' he said.

I pointed at his necklace. 'Did you tackle a shark for that?'

He grinned, baring his teeth. 'I *am* the shark.'

He dived underwater and grabbed my ankles, pulling me off balance. I went under, water going up my nose. I flailed around, arms churning, legs kicking, trying to find a footing. When I came up for air, he was laughing at me. I was so angry. *What a dumbass!*

His smile quickly faded when he realised how upset I was. 'Sorry,' he said, swimming up close to me. 'I was just stuffing around. I didn't mean to scare you. Are you okay?'

I wasn't about to let him know he'd totally freaked me out. 'It was a just a surprise, is all,' I said, pinching my dripping nose. 'I'm fine.'

He looked towards the house. There was no sign of Dene. 'Tully...' he said quietly.

'Yeah?'

He looked right into my eyes and his foot touched mine. 'Do you think I could have your number?'

I must've been looking at him like he was crazy, because he added, 'You know...if things don't work out with Dene.'

Oh my god!

I was about to tell him that he was a royal jerk and I would *never* do that to my friend, but Dene came outside and put her phone on the table and, with a running leap, she dive-bombed into the pool. Coops swam straight over to her. He grabbed her by her waist and swung her around. She squealed with laughter.

I felt sick. I'd *have* to tell her. A good friend would tell, right?

I climbed out of the pool and grabbed my towel.

'Tully!' Dene yelled. 'Where are you going?'

I rubbed my stomach. 'I don't feel so great.'

She pushed Coops away and swam over to me. 'Have you got it?' she whispered.

'Huh?'

She looked over her shoulder at Coops, then back at me. 'Your period. I can get you a tampon if you want?'

'Oh. No. I don't think so.' But then I thought about it. If she thought I had it, she'd have to come to the bathroom with me. 'Actually, maybe I do,' I said.

'Back in a minute!' Dene called. She climbed out of the pool. 'Give me your towel.' I handed it to her and she dried herself off. 'This way,' she said.

I followed her inside, trying not to slip on the shiny white tiles. She went to go to the bathroom, but I grabbed her arm, stopping her in the kitchen.

She turned to look at me. 'What?'

I blurted it out fast, 'Coops asked for my number.'

She stared at me like I was speaking Swedish.

'When you were inside,' I said.

I waited for her to thank me, to say Coops was a creep and best friends ruled the earth, but her nose wrinkled up as if she smelled something bad.

'So?' she snapped.

'I—'

'You know he's just being nice, right?'

'Well I—'

'*Right?*'

'Right,' I said.

With a lingering glare, she marched past me, back out to the pool.

I called to her. She ignored me.

'False alarm!' Dene said. 'Tully thought she had her period but she doesn't.' She turned and smiled sweetly at me.

I looked at everyone's faces, horrified.

'Mads is coming over soon, Tully,' Dene added. 'Hope you don't mind.' She slid herself into the pool, swum over to Coops and splashed him. 'You're going down!' she cried, before launching herself at him, trying to dunk him.

After that it was like I'd disappeared.

When Michelle and Luke picked me up a couple of hours later, I was glad to leave.

Luke was driving. He was on his L's and he needed to get his hours up.

'Your chauffeur,' he said in a posh voice as I got into the back seat, 'reporting to the princess for duty.'

'Shut up,' I said. I was not in the mood for his stupid jokes.

'Did you take any groundbreaking selfies today?' he asked, pulling out of Dene's driveway. He mimicked Dene in a girly voice, '*Oh no! My hair got wet! What will I do? Quick, someone take a photo and record this earth-shattering moment!*'

'I said *Shut up!*'

'Cool it, Luke,' Michelle said. 'Focus on driving, please.'

But Luke went on. 'Did you hear about the influencer who took a photo at the top of a cliff?'

'No,' I said, digging around in my bag for my phone. 'But let me guess: you're going to tell me.'

'This dude was taking a selfie at the Grand Canyon,' Luke said. 'He was at the cliff's edge and he stepped backwards trying to get as close as he could, and he started to lose his footing and go over, so he grabbed his friend to pull him back up, and they both went down together, plunging to the bottom of a deep ravine. *Dead.* Dead from taking a selfie.'

Michelle gasped. 'That's horrible!'

'Urban myth,' I said, finding my phone.

'Is not!' Luke protested.

'Pity you didn't fall down a deep ravine,' I said.

'Turn left here,' Michelle instructed.

Luke turned. 'Did you record your afternoon snack, Tully? Let me guess. Was it oven-baked camembert cheese with pomegranate juice and yoghurt-lime dressing? How can I possibly get through the rest of my life without knowing that?'

'I haven't posted anything!' I said, happy it was the truth.

'What about what you were wearing?' Luke kept on. 'What label was it? I'll have to jump online and order it in my size.'

Michelle smirked.

'Nothing comes in your size!' I said, kicking the back of his seat. 'You're too fat!'

'Tully!' Michelle gasped, swinging around in her seat to look at me. 'That's not very nice. Take that back.'

'And *he* is being nice?'

The car suddenly swerved. Michelle switched her focus back to Luke. She grasped at the steering wheel as if to right the vehicle.

With a heavy sigh, she rested her elbow on the door's windowsill, forehead pressed to her hand. 'You two are going to be the death of me. Luke, *please* concentrate. I don't want another injury. One is more than enough. And if you two could just call it a truce for this car ride, that would be most appreciated.'

'Gladly!' I agreed.

'Fine,' Luke said.

I opened Insta. Dene had posted a few minutes ago. It was a photo of Coops's torso—no head, no board shorts, just his dripping wet chest.

Guess who? Some secrets stay secrets. #dene-queens #walkwithmewalker #ncwalker #youngandfree #livingthedream

I was furious. She hadn't even posted an anonymous shot of me yet! (Well, other than my hand and my wrist.) I don't know what I was more angry about: the fact she hadn't believed me when I'd told her about Coops, or that she'd told him I might have my period, *or* that she'd invited me over and spent most of the afternoon ignoring me and hanging out with Coops and Maddy instead.

I didn't even get to confirm if she was coming to the movies for my birthday.

How is it a day could start out full of happiness and end like this?

I checked if Kira had responded to my message about Art the other day, but she hadn't. *Nothing.*

I fired off a text, feeling grumpy and not really caring about how I worded it: Where are you? Black hole much?

Kira texted back straightaway: Thought you were too busy

I felt like sending a string of question marks and red cranky faces, but instead I kept a lid on it and wrote: I checked on you—I wasn't too busy to do that

It was a couple of minutes before she wrote back: True. Sorry. Talk soon about Drama class, huh? 😊

Me: 😊

But I didn't feel like smiling *or* winking.

And I *still* had to tell her that I didn't want to do it.

Later that night, Dene DM'd me: I asked Coops. He said he just wanted to stay in touch cos you're my friend.

I thought about it, suddenly feeling unsure. *What if I'd got it wrong?*

Me: K

Dene: I forgive you

That irked me. It should be *me* forgiving *her*. But I felt a smile on my lips even though I was still mad at her. She was trying to make it right.

I love-hearted her comment.

Me: Movies tomorrow?

I watched the icon move down.

She left me on read. *Again.*

CHAPTER TWELVE

#BirthdayBlues

I checked my phone as soon as I woke up. Kira had DM'd a pic of a monkey's bum.

Kira: Happy birthday to you. You live in a zoo. You look like a monkey's bum and you act like one too.

I laughed. She could be so juvenile. But I kinda liked that about her.

Me: Love the pic. Selfie?

Kira: Ah! Your stand-up career awaits. But seriously, I downloaded it from Dene's newsfeed

Me: 😆 Now who's the comedian?

Kira: Wanna hang out?

Me: Maybe. I'll let you know

Kira: 😞

I felt yuck for saying that, and I knew Kira could only keep forgiving me for so long, but I wanted to know what Dene was doing. Were we going to the movies?

I checked for messages from Dene but there was nothing. It was only 7.30 am. She was probably still asleep. She'd get to it. Maybe she'd saved up all those photos she'd taken of us to do a birthday post?

Happy Birthday to the most amazing friend on earth. Tully Sinclair is my world. #bffs #denequeens #walkwithmewalker #ncwalker #youngandfree #livingthedream

I went to the loo, taking my phone with me, and I almost dropped it in the toilet. I did that once with my house keys. I peed, and I realised there was no choice but to stick my hand in there and get them. I used, like, a *whole* container of pump soap after that.

I took a shower, keeping the glass door open, my arm outstretched and holding my phone. If Michelle saw me reading posts like that she would've gone bonkers. She's caught me before. The bathmat gets soaked and she gets cranky. Someone needs to invent waterproof phones for showers and toilets, I swear.

I watched my birthday wishes rolling in, hoping to see Dene's name. I didn't care about the other people saying nice things. I knew that made me a terrible, ungrateful person, and maybe I was, but it was the truth. I honestly didn't care.

After putting on trackies and a T-shirt, I walked

into the kitchen with my hair wrapped in a towel.

Michelle was making pancakes. 'Topping?' she asked.

'Lemon-sugar.'

'Mickey Mouse shaped?'

I laughed. 'What am I? Ten?'

She looked at her watch. 'Fourteen, according to today's calendar. Happy birthday, lovely girl.'

'Thanks.' I sat at the dining table. After a minute or so, she brought over my plate. I looked down at it, then at her. 'What the—?'

My pancakes were round with strategically placed cream and raspberry garnish that looked suspiciously like—

'Boobs,' Michelle confirmed.

'Um, *why?*'

'You're fourteen. Time to move on from Mickey Mouse. Why not celebrate your femininity?'

'I hope you're not going to make Luke's shaped like a—'

'I'll have the boobs special too, thanks,' Luke said, plopping himself down next to me. 'Make them extra large.' His hair was a dirty mop and he was wearing *Star Wars* boxer shorts. He leant back in his chair and scratched an armpit.

I held my nose. 'Need a map to get to the bathroom?'

'Some selfish teenage girl was hogging it.' He plunged a hand into his boxers and gave that a good scratch too.

I cringed. 'Could you not?'

He pulled a small square package from his boxers that was wrapped in newspaper. He chucked it on the table. 'Happy Birthday,' he said.

I prodded it with the tip of my finger—it *had* been inside his shorts. 'How thoughtful, Luke. Nice wrapping. I don't know what to say.'

'Open it.' He grabbed my fork, carved off a piece of my pancake and snaffled it.

'Hey!' I snatched back my fork. 'Get your own boobs!'

I opened his gift. It was his official school photo. He'd framed it.

He waggled a finger at me. 'Just be careful. If you throw darts at it, the glass will break.'

'And that's a problem *because?*'

'I wanted to give you something to remind you of the VIPs in your life.' He sat back, smug.

My phone buzzed and my heart leapt with the thought it could be Dene.

It was Dad.

Luke rolled his eyes when he saw my flashing screen. 'Don't tell me,' he said. 'Dad's announcing he's on the six o'clock flight just in time for the last dregs of your birthday.'

I slapped him. 'Shut up.' I put Dad on speaker. 'Hey, Dad.'

'Happy Birthday, Button!' Dad yelled so loud the phone crackled. If he was at an airport, it would've been crazy embarrassing. Imagine some guy in the Qantas lounge yelling that in your ear?

I laughed. 'Thanks, Dad.'

'I transferred some money to your account,' he said. 'Go shopping. Buy yourself something frivolous.'

Michelle was listening. She mouthed *frivolous* and pulled a *what-the* face at me.

'Are you coming home?' I asked.

'Nah. Sorry. Big one on the hook. Gotta reel him in.'

I was careful not to look disappointed in front of Luke and Michelle—they did enough of that for me.

'All good,' I said, like it didn't matter.

'That's my Button!' There was a rustling noise. Dad was obviously looking through papers. 'You don't happen to have me on speaker, do you?'

Luke and Michelle looked like a pair of mimes, frantically waving their hands, shaking their heads and sliding their fingers across their throats.

'No,' I lied.

'Okay.' He sounded disappointed. 'Hey, let me know if you hear from your mum, huh?'

I swallowed. We both knew *that* wasn't going to happen. 'Yep. Sure thing, Dad.'

'Have a happy day,' he said. 'I'll check your Insta for birthday pics. Hey, on that note, I saw that drawing you put up. Who's the girl?'

He'd seen the one of Dene. 'That's my best friend,' I said proudly. 'She's kind of famous.' I said that because of what Dad does for a living—he hangs out with famous people. I knew it would impress him.

Luke rolled his eyes at me. He did it so often, I wondered if he'd pull a muscle and end up stuck like that. 'Famous in her own lunchbox,' he muttered.

'Well, it's a very good drawing, honey,' Dad said. 'You have your mother's talent.'

That made my skin prickle. 'I have *my* talent,' I said.

Dad gave an uneasy chuckle. 'Of course you do.' I heard the paper shuffling noise again. 'Whoops. I'd better go. Tell Michelle I'll call her later. And say hi to Luke for me.'

'Sure. Okay. Love you.'

'Love you too, Button.'

Dad hung up.

'What an A-class—' Luke began to say.

'*Luke!*' Michelle said, shaking her head.

'At least he rang,' I said.

They both knew I was really referring to Mum. To his credit, Luke didn't say anything about that.

'Well I guess that's the Tully lovefest over for the day,' Luke said, brushing his hands. 'Time to get back to the important people.'

I stood up, untangled my towel and shook my dripping-wet hair all over him.

He put up his hands. 'Ew! Girl germs!' Then he grabbed my fork and stole another piece of pancake.

'Don't worry,' Michelle said to me. 'I'll cook you some more, Tully. And for the record, it wasn't that I didn't want to speak to your father, I just didn't want to talk to him *right now*. I'm cooking. I don't want to burn the house down.'

'I know,' I said. But I also knew that whatever Michelle wanted to say to Dad, she wanted to say in private—which meant it couldn't be anything good.

'Oh! I almost forgot!' Michelle went into the lounge and came back with a large package wrapped in purple-and-white spotty paper. She handed it to me. 'Happy birthday, darling girl!'

I tore off the wrapping. It was a wooden desktop art easel much like the one Dene had had in her photo.

I stood up and hugged her. 'I love it, Michelle!

Thank you!'

Michelle winced. 'Careful, careful...not too hard.' She rubbed her back. 'I'm glad you like it. I look forward to seeing more of your artwork, Tully. Maybe a portrait of someone closer to home?' She turned side-on, cupping her cheeks, pouting her lips in a dramatic pose.

I laughed. 'Okay. Maybe.'

Luke snorted, 'Don't bother drawing me. Picasso rang. He's doing me next week.'

'From the grave,' I said. 'Impressive.'

We ate pancakes and joked around some more. As birthday breakfasts go, it wasn't at all bad. Michelle and Luke could be all right sometimes.

I even forgot to check my phone.

But at 11 am I was starting to get worried. I paced my bedroom, constantly refreshing my phone and my laptop for updates. Still nothing from Dene. Then again there were no Insta posts from her either. Maybe she was busy. I didn't know exactly how long Coops and his dad were staying, but maybe she was saying her farewells and then she was going to call me.

My fingers hovered over the keypad. Should I message her? It was *my* birthday. She should be messaging me. But I really wanted to know if we were going to the movies.

I decided I was being stupid. She was my friend. What difference did it make if I sent a message? People do it every day.

Me: Hey Dene. Just wondering if we're still on for the movies?

I hit send. There. Done. She had to get back to me now. She'd see that and remember my birthday.

Two hours later, I was still waiting. Kira had messaged again, asking what was happening. Michelle had been to my room twice to check on me. I told her I was planning to go out with friends and I was just waiting for them to confirm where we were meeting. She accepted that, but she looked concerned.

I sat on my bed, reading Insta posts. Maddy had posted a pic of some random record store in the city that I'd never been to. The post had gone up two minutes ago. My stomach lurched when I saw Dene had commented: So cool. I def wanna go there with you next time.

She was online!

If Maddy had only just posted, did that mean Dene would message me next? Then I realised I'd sent her an actual text two hours ago—*not* a DM. She didn't have to be online to see it. It would've gone straight through.

Was she ignoring me? Was this about Coops? I

thought she was over that? What if it was just an oversight and she hadn't seen my message at all? What if the stupid phone company said my message was delivered when really it was out there looping Saturn and Neptune? Argh! I should've sent it to her on an app where I could *see* whether she'd seen it.

Another hour ticked by. It was now 2 pm. Half of the day had gone. Pretty soon Michelle wouldn't be letting me go anywhere.

I gave up and messaged Kira: Movies?

Kira: *squeeeeeeeeeeeeeeeee* Meet ya there

I told myself that if Dene messaged I'd work something out. I'd make up an excuse and cancel with Kira.

I had a gnawing feeling *again* like I was a horrible person.

I ignored it.

Kira and I went and saw the tornado movie. We had a nice time, but I couldn't concentrate on the film or on what Kira was talking about. I kept drifting off, thinking about Dene and why she hadn't messaged me back. Kira didn't seem to notice. She was too busy cracking jokes and eating candy-bar food. I made sure I nodded and said things in the right places. *Uh-huh. Oh, that's funny. You're kidding!* But I was only half-listening to her. I wanted to laugh, to be in the moment, but I wasn't. I also visited the bathroom about ten times. Kira *did* ask about that. I told her I might have a bladder infection. Not that I know what bladder infections do to you, but it sounded highly probable. In truth, I only needed to go twice. The other times I locked myself in a cubicle and checked my socials.

When I got home, Kira sent me a beautiful message telling me what a great time she'd had. I messaged back a string of love hearts, but *my* heart wasn't really in it. I also did something completely gutless and seized the moment to say I'd forgotten to tell her I didn't want to do drama group. She'd tried to ask me about it when we were out, but I'd dodged the question and changed the subject. It was a few minutes before she texted back. When she did, she just said: Ok. No problem ☹

I knew it *was* a problem, but I decided not to say any more. She'd get over it.

I said goodnight to Michelle, cleaned my teeth and went to bed. I kept checking my phone until midnight.

Zilch.

Nada.

Zip.

As twelve o'clock ticked over, I realised Mum hadn't messaged me either. I'd been too focused on

Dene to even think about her.

Everything inside me sank. I wasn't worth it to either of them.

CHAPTER THIRTEEN

#WorstConclusion

Michelle called my I've-got-a-stomach-ache bluff on Monday morning. She was ready for me like one of those TV reporters on the steps outside of a court-house, firing questions thick and fast. It's a miracle she didn't wave a microphone in my face.

'You were online half the night, Tully. What were you doing?'

I decided a non-combative approach would be best. I didn't want her to think I was in a bad mood—which I was. That would result in even more questions.

I mustered a smile. 'I assume *No comment* isn't going to cut it?'

She held up her phone. 'I have evidence.'

I went to protest, but like any good reporter she'd done her research. She'd taken screenshots of the icons indicating I'd been online. I tried to tell her I'd left the apps open, but she wasn't buying it. I had also stupidly commented on someone's status at 2 am. (This is how crime detectives track down modern-day axe-murderers, I swear.)

'Final warning,' Michelle said, arching her back and wincing with the pain of it. 'If you can't be trusted to stay off your phone and sleep when you should be sleeping, I'll be confiscating it every night.'

I looked at one of her pictures. 'Hang on. What were *you* doing online at that time?' I leaned in close to see the tabs she'd had open. I spied the website *Iconic*. 'Hmmm. Bit of late-night retail therapy?'

Michelle closed the screen. 'I'm an adult, Tully. I can manage my time how I see fit. You have school and you need your sleep.'

'I get plenty of sleep during coding class.'

'Be serious.'

I could tell she didn't appreciate my wit. I stretched and yawned. 'Look, I won't do it again.'

She raised an eyebrow. 'I'm pretty sure the record shows you've said that before.'

'This time I mean it.'

'So said every other offender.'

'You have a law degree,' I argued. 'You're supposed to believe in reform.'

She went to the kitchen and poured me a mug of

coffee. 'Here,' she said, passing it to me. 'Caffeine. Suck it in long and deep, young friend. You're going to need it.' She pointed at the pile of dishes. 'You can reform with these.'

On the bus to school I almost threw up. It was because I was going to see Dene. I was panicking about what to say. I could try to act normal but I already knew it wouldn't work. I'd take one look at her and burst into tears.

How could my best friend miss my birthday?

But here's something weird: if anyone else had done that to me, I would've got so mad I wouldn't have spoken to them for ages. If it was Kira, I would've gone full bananas and told her what I really thought. With Dene? I already knew it would be different. I wasn't sure why.

I checked Dene's Insta. There was a post of her in the shower, grinning at the camera over her bare shoulder, holding up a bottle of shampoo that said *Hair Bear Stares* on the label. Her hair was soaped into a lopsided Mohawk. She had foamy eyebrows and a frothy-bearded chin.

Bubble bubble boil and trouble. No trouble here! This stuff rocks. #denequeens #walkwithme-walker #ncwalker #youngandfree #livingthedream

*#shampoo #buynow #hairbearstares #getyourstareon
#bearhugsforyourhair*

The comments ranged from *Ordering some right now!* to *You're so gorgeous!* to *Funny as well as cute!* I read them, feeling sicker. If she had time to post about shampoo *and* to reply to Maddy, why didn't she have time for me?

I scrolled through Dene's earlier posts—the ones from before I knew her in real life. She wasn't like the other influencers who posted perfect gym bodies contorted into yoga poses set against glorious beach sunsets. Or the ones who wore designer dresses and had a guy with a dentist's-dream gleaming smile hanging off their arm. Dene's feed was the full rainbow of emotions: happy, miserable, disappointed, elated, nervous, confident, afraid, fearless—and against all kinds of backdrops: in the car, at the movies, the supermarket, her bedroom, a takeaway restaurant, a playground. She posted with and without make-up. She posted when she'd just woken up, her hair a tousled mess, face still sleep-scrunched. She posted at the doctor's surgery with a blood-pressure cuff on her arm. She posted scrubbing the car or plucking lint from the clothes dryer. I felt like I had a connection with her: a clear window into her life and who she was. It was like she wasn't hiding anything.

But she was hiding something.

Me.

At least it felt that way—and that was a familiar feeling.

I flicked my camera to the download album and scrolled until I found my favourite photo of Mum. Dad had taken it at one of her early exhibitions.

Mum was standing under a spotlight pointing to a dark, foreboding painting with haphazard blocks of black, grey, blue and purple. Its erratic nature made me think of a messy mind. Mum was wearing a white tank-top with red overalls, army boots, colourful jewellery and thick black eyeliner. Her blonde hair was wrapped in a green scarf. A crowd watched her, holding champagne glasses, laughing at something she was saying.

I remember that exhibition even though I was only seven or eight. Luke and I had to stay in a dedicated kids area. I remember being annoyed about it. Why couldn't we walk around and look at the art, too? We were given paper and textas and told to make our own art.

Luke never drew anything. He just played Super Mario on his Nintendo.

I drew the gallery as a map—room after room, with little squares on the walls for paintings, glass cases holding pottery vases, sculptures on plinths, even security guards by the doors. I was so proud of it. It took hours—*all* the hours that exhibition dragged on. I spent that time thinking about what Mum would say when she saw it.

When the party ended and Dad came to collect us, Mum was still talking to people and answering questions about her next exhibition. I tugged on her arm for at least a minute before she finally looked down at me and said in a snippy voice, *What is it, Tully?* I held up my drawing. She barely glanced at it. She just said *That's great* and patted my hand. Then she told Dad to take me home; she was going to a bar with friends to celebrate.

I cried all the way home. I asked Dad why Mum didn't like my picture.

She's just busy, Tully. It's hard for her to focus. Tonight wasn't about us. It was about her. She wasn't your mum tonight. She was a star.

I couldn't understand what he meant. All I understood was that Mum wasn't my mum. Like it was a choice. Like it was something you can switch on and off. She'd hidden us away as if we didn't exist. We weren't important like those other people.

I closed the screen. My phone buzzed and a notification popped up.

Dene: What's taking you so long? Hurry up. Things to tell.

I stared at it. *Huh?* No mention of my text or my birthday. Maybe my text did get delivered to some other planet?

Dene was waiting for me at the bus stop, head down looking at her phone. When she saw me, she picked up her school bag and bounded over, freshly blow-dried hair swinging across her shoulders. That Bear shampoo stuff looked good—not that I was going to tell her that. I'd vowed to be icy, to not give too much away. Not until I knew why she'd blown me off.

She moaned, 'I've been waiting for you for, like, *forever.*' When I didn't say anything, she added, 'I've had the worst time!'

Despite myself, I took the bait. 'Why's that?'

She rolled her eyes. 'Coops.'

'What about him?'

She grabbed my hand and ran her thumb over my bluebird ring. 'You were right. I'm not sure he's the nicest guy.'

The ice-cap inside me began to melt. 'Why? What'd he do?'

'We had an argument,' she said. Before I could ask what about, she moved on. 'And Mum cracked it at me because I hadn't done her post about the shampoo. Remember that one that was delivered the night you came for a sleepover? I'd forgotten all about it. The company sent Mum a *Please Explain* email and she went ballistic at me and told me to do it straight-away.' Dene stopped to give Maddy a quick wave. 'And then I was at the supermarket with Mum and I spilled chocolate milk on my white shorts and you can imagine what that looked like. This old man pulled a disgusted face and it was *so* embarrassing. But that wasn't even the worst thing!'

My ice-cap had fully liquified. I was fast on a path to global warming. '*It wasn't?*'

'No. Dad called. He's getting married.'

'What?'

'And having a baby.'

I blinked. I couldn't believe it. No wonder she didn't have time for me! 'Oh my god, Dene!'

'Oh! And here...' She stopped, dug around in her bag, pulled out an envelope and handed it to me. 'This is for you.'

I opened it. It was a card that said *Happy Birthday to My Best Friend* in gold letters. On the inside she'd written, *We're gunna have an awesome time today. Love you.* Stuck to the other side was a movie voucher.

Her eyes were on her sneakers. 'I'm so sorry, Tully. I feel terrible.'

I felt tears coming—tears of relief. Why'd I think all those bad things? Why did I jump to the worst possible conclusion?

Then I remembered her comment on Maddy's post.

'It's okay,' I said gently. 'I just wondered why you didn't send me a quick message to explain?'

She scuffed her sneakers on the footpath. 'I was going to, but I wanted to make it a good one. You know...put some effort into it. Every time I sat down to do it, I couldn't. I didn't want to screw it up. I wanted it to be perfect.' She looked right at me and added, 'Sometimes wanting to be perfect is what stops me, you know? It's like I'm stuck. If it's not perfect, there's no point.'

I wanted to tell her about how I'd worried myself sick, about how I'd cried when she didn't respond, about the hours I spent waiting, but I couldn't find the right words. I also wondered what good it would do. She couldn't go back and change it. She really was sorry. And she had thought about me on my birthday She'd obviously written the card days ago.

I put my arm around her. 'It's okay, Dene. Do you want to talk about it?'

We walked to class, with Dene telling me all about

her dad; about all the other stuff in her life that was weighing her down. All the disappointment I'd felt evaporated. Things were as they were before. Normal.

CHAPTER FOURTEEN

#UnderTheInfluence

TV matchmaking shows talk about wedded bliss. I don't know what the term for *friendship bliss* is, but the following week was exactly that.

Monday after school: Dene and I did our homework together in the library.

Tuesday lunchtime: we taught the latest TikTok dance craze to the whole of year eight.

Wednesday: we skipped PE, hid in the cleaner's room and shared a can of Pringles.

Thursday: detention. (See Pringles.)

Friday: after begging Michelle and Kaz (see also Pringles/Detention), we went to the movies to make up for missing out on my birthday.

The movie had a foreign name I couldn't pronounce and it was about something highly improbable featuring sharks, planes and oversized fang-toothed arachnids. We were too busy joking around to care anyway.

We sat at the back of the cinema, arms linked, feeding each other M&Ms and Doritos. We made a pact that only the other person could 'feed and water' you. It was hilarious. Half a packet of M&Ms went down my top and I wore most of my Fanta. Dene licked Doritos dust from my fingers. I accidentally missed her mouth with the straw and it went up her nose. She sneezed, like, *ten times*. People turned in their seats to scowl, but we didn't care. We were having way too much fun.

That night, Dene slept over at my house. Despite Luke's assertions Dene wasn't any kind of influence on him, he acted like he was *under the influence* when he met her. He actually stuttered when he said *Hello,* and he wouldn't stop staring at her.

Dene was cool about it. Afterwards she told me that Luke was kind of cute in an awkward loser sort of way.

I wasn't sure whether to bank that as a compliment or an insult.

When everyone was in bed, we lay side-by-side in our sleeping bags on a mattress on the lounge-room floor. Michelle said we could watch TV if we kept our voices down.

The TV flickered, sound low. Dene twisted her body to face me. She was about to say something, but right when she opened her mouth my phone flashed. I checked the message.

Kira: You'd make a good disappearing act.

'Who's that?' Dene asked, probably seeing me frown.

'Kira.'

'And?'

'Nothing.' I tucked my phone down the side of the mattress.

'Doesn't look like nothing.'

I shrugged it off. 'I haven't seen her much lately, that's all. She'll get over it.'

'We should invite her to do something with us,' Dene suggested kindly. 'She's a good friend of yours. I hardly know her.'

'Maybe...' I said, uncommitted. I didn't particularly want to share Dene even if it would make Kira happy.

When I didn't say anything else, Dene changed the subject. 'Have your heard from your mum, Tully?'

Since I'd told Dene about Mum's illness, I hadn't thought about it. But the fact that Dene remembered made me feel good all over again.

Totally aware I was being a drama queen, I

answered in a deliberately shaky voice, 'No, I haven't heard from her.'

'Oh, I'm so sorry...' Dene said.

A year ago, Michelle took me to a day spa for some girly pampering. We had a sauna and a massage, a pedicure and manicure, and a wash and blow-dry. We wore fluffy white bathrobes and we sat in reclining chairs and sipped green smoothies and ate Buddha bowls surrounded by candles and soothing background music. Afterwards, it felt like someone had pressed my Snooze button. Every single cell in my body was totally chilled.

A few caring words from Dene had the same effect.

She stroked my cheek, her eyes glistening. 'Your mum doesn't know what she's missing.'

I took her hand, lacing her fingers with mine. 'Dene?'

'Yeah?'

'Do you think it's weird that you can not know a person and be perfectly fine, but then you meet that person and you don't want to live without them?'

Her eyebrows knitted. 'I'm not sure I get what you mean?'

I tried to explain. 'Before I knew you in real life, if someone had said to me *unfollow her, don't look,* I probably could've done that. But now I know you and we've spent so much time together, switching off is impossible. I don't want to. I don't want to be without you.'

A smile crept over her face. She squeezed my hand tight. 'Remember your bluebird ring, Tully? We're sisters now. Girls who stick together. No one can break that.'

I wanted to believe her more than anything.

'True,' Dene insisted.

I pulled my hand away. 'What about Maddy?'

'What about her?'

I needed to know. I *had* to know. 'Am *I* your best friend?'

Dene adjusted her pillow, doubling it over, tucking her hands beneath. 'Of course.' But her voice was tight. 'I gave you a card that said so. Why are you asking?'

I bit my lip, realising I didn't really know why I was asking. Maybe because I couldn't quite believe she liked me for real.

'You're kind of freaking me out, Tully,' Dene said.

I stared at her.

She rolled onto her back and looked at the ceiling. 'A girl at my old school acted like this.'

I swallowed, not knowing what to say. 'I'm sorry, I didn't mean to—'

'Her name was Amelia,' Dene said. 'We were friends, but then things became...*weird*. She followed me around at school and online. And before you say that's what friends do, this was different. It was over the top.'

'I'm not like that,' I whispered.

'This girl bought the *exact* same clothes as me,' Dene said. 'If I got pink hair extensions, so did she. If I posted about going to the beach on Saturday, there'd be a post of her at the beach on Sunday. She'd go to the same cafes as me, buy the same fruit juices as me, even see the same movies and read the same books as me. If I said that pizza was my favourite food, she'd write a favourable review all about pizza. She copied *everything* I did.'

'I don't do that,' I said.

She inhaled deeply. 'No, you don't. But what happened makes me nervous.'

Something in the pit of my stomach felt like it was burning. *Was I like this Amelia girl?*

Dene rolled over to face me. 'I'm here with you, aren't I?'

I didn't understand.

'I wouldn't be here if I didn't want to be,' Dene said.

I nodded. 'Okay. It's just...'

'What?' She sounded impatient.

I hesitated, then I decided to spit it out. 'There are so many people saying nice stuff about you, Dene. So many people wanting to be your friend. I don't get it. Why me?'

She shrugged. 'Why not you?'

Tears stung my eyes. There were countless reasons *Why not me*. I wasn't good enough. I wasn't pretty enough. I wasn't rich enough. My parents didn't care enough. My brother thought I was a pain in the backside. My teachers didn't think I was anything special. No one really cared when I put stuff online. Hardly anyone commented or liked it. I was basically a loser. And I didn't know how to say any of that out loud.

Dene lovingly tapped my nose. 'I like you, Tully Sinclair. That should be enough.'

She was right. It should've been.

Kaz picked Dene up early the next morning. Michelle and Luke were still in bed. We hadn't even had breakfast yet. Dene was meant to stay till late afternoon, but Kaz sent her a message and told her she had to come home.

That's what Dene told me.

I watched her pack her things. 'Do you really have to go?'

'Yeah. Business stuff,' she said.

'Can't it wait?'

She rolled her eyes. 'People think it's easy doing what I do, Tully, but it's actually hard work. Mum did a marketing and communications course and she's really hot on following what she learned. Regular posting is key to building an audience.'

I wanted to say she already had a huge audience; that *I* was her real-life audience, but instead I asked, 'What are you selling today?'

She shrugged. 'Dunno. Guess I'll find out.'

'Don't you get sick of it?'

She rubbed her forehead. 'Sometimes. Yeah. Most of the time. But it is what it is.'

I dug my thumbnail into the palm of my hand so hard it stung.

'What's wrong?' she asked, watching me.

'You could stop,' I said.

She looked at me like I was crazy.

'I've stopped,' I said. 'I've gone months without posting anything. You don't have to do it if you don't want to.'

She zipped up her bag. 'That's *you*. You're not a big deal.' When she saw how that statement wounded me, she quickly said, 'You know what I mean, Tully.'

'No, no, it's okay. It's true. I'm not.' *I definitely*

wasn't a big deal. I was a nobody.

She sighed. 'Don't do this.'

'Do what?'

'Act like this.' She slung her bag over her shoulder.

'I'm just trying to tell you that it's a choice.'

'People who say stuff like that *have* choices,' Dene said stiffly.

But I kept on at her, not wanting for her to be unhappy. 'Have you thought about what things would be like if you didn't—'

She looked at her phone. 'Sorry. I have to go. Mum's out the front. Thanks for having me.' She headed to the door, then stopped and turned to look at me. Her eyes were cloudy. 'You know, I thought you understood, Tully.'

'I do—'

She cut me off. 'Sounds like it.'

'I was just trying to—'

'Here's a tip,' she said in a snippy voice. 'Sort out your own life before you go trying to fix mine.' She walked out.

My chest caved and my insides cracked in half. I started crying and couldn't stop.

Michelle came rushing out when she heard.

'Tully?' she gasped, wrapping her arms around me. 'What happened? Are you all right?'

I sobbed.

'Come,' she said, steering me to the kitchen. 'I'll put the kettle on.'

I sat down at the table and howled. Michelle didn't let it faze her. She did her thing, making coffee and cereal while I cried and cried.

'There,' she said, putting breakfast in front of me.

I pushed it aside. I didn't want to eat. I wanted to throw up.

'You girls obviously had an argument,' Michelle said. 'Tell me about it. Maybe I can help.'

I looked at her, hopeful. I was willing to take all the help I could get. 'I tried to tell Dene that she doesn't need to put stuff online,' I said.

Michelle nodded. 'I see. And she didn't take that well, huh?'

I shook my head.

She sipped her coffee. 'We're good at this, us humans.'

'Huh?'

'We like someone, *love* someone, and then we try to change them,' Michelle said.

'But it's making her unhappy!'

'Your dad does things that make him unhappy,' Michelle said. 'Try telling him that.'

I grabbed my mug and pulled it towards me. 'We're

not talking about Dad.'

'No, we're not,' Michelle agreed. 'But we could be. Same thing, really.'

'No, it's not,' I said. But deep down I knew what she was getting at.

'You can't change people, Tully,' Michelle said. 'People are who they choose to be until they choose to be something different.'

I half-snorted. 'Dene said she doesn't have a *choice*.'

'Maybe she doesn't.'

'She said her mum wants her to do stuff online. Can't she tell her no?'

Michelle smiled. 'You're assuming that because you can confidently say no to me that Dene can do the same.'

'Kaz is nice,' I said. 'She'd understand.'

Michelle's eyebrows shot up. 'Kaz started this posting bizzo! From what I can tell—and before you ask, *I did look her up*—Kaz has been posting about Dene since before Dene was born. Dene has grown up with this stuff. She doesn't know any different. She's never been given a choice. This is a business to Kaz. They make money from what they sell and Dene is the product.'

I knew that, of course, but until Michelle spelled it out, I hadn't thought hard about how long things had been this way.

'Look at their car. Look at their clothes! You think these things are free, but there's a cost. An *emotional* cost.'

It was true. And the longer I thought about it, the more it made sense. I was blinded by the stuff Dene was receiving, not seeing what she was giving in return.

Michelle straightened her dressing-gown, then she tucked her hair behind her ears. 'Do you want to hear something really honest, Tully?'

I nodded.

'Personally, I don't think much of parents who choose to exploit their kids. To me, that's what it is: exploitation. It's not giving the child a choice, nor a true voice. I actually think Kaz is quite selfish.'

'But Dene has a voice,' I said, confused. 'She's the one doing the posts.'

Michelle tipped her head at me, a look on her face like I should be smarter than that.

'With her mum standing over her?' I said slowly.

Michelle smiled. 'Exactly. In my opinion, children—*especially* those too young to make choices for themselves—should not be put in that position. One day those children grow up—like Dene—and what then?'

It suddenly made sense. Dene is of an age where she could start making decisions for herself, but she also wasn't—at least not legally. She was caught somewhere in the middle.

'I know there are bloggers who keep their children's privacy by using pseudonyms,' Michelle said, 'and I think that's a respectful way of going about things. Or they only ever post photos of the back of their kids' heads. But Dene was never given that option, was she.'

I shook my head. 'No.'

'So this online world of hers...this artificial world... it's become her real world, too. One bleeds into the other.' Michelle reached across the table for my hand and patted it. 'I know you were looking out for your friend, Tully. But this isn't as simple as you might think. It's actually very complicated—for Dene *and* for her mum.'

I wiped away tears. Michelle was right.

'What should I do now?' I asked.

Michelle smiled. 'Be there for Dene as a friend. Give her support. Don't offer solutions. Let her do her thing and let her talk to you when she needs to. She's muddling through as best she can. Eventually she'll figure it out. In the meantime, try not to judge her. Things may look easy from the outside but they rarely ever are.'

I nodded. Michelle made me think of something. Ms Brian once said: *Everyone you know is grappling with something. The best we can do is be kind to one another.* I needed to remember that.

Michelle ruffled my hair. 'You're a smart girl, Tully. You're sweet and compassionate. Dene is very lucky to have you for a friend.'

Michelle might have seen it that way, but I didn't know if I did. I felt like a bad friend. *Why didn't I stop to think about all that stuff Michelle just explained?*

'Hey...' Michelle eyeballed me. 'I can see that brain of yours ticking. Don't blame yourself. Move forward with a better plan, eh?'

I liked that—a better plan.

'I'm sure Dene will understand,' Michelle reassured.

I hoped so. Because if she didn't, I didn't know what I'd do.

Probably stay in bed and cry for the next century.

CHAPTER FIFTEEN

#CrackedHeart

On Monday morning I felt strangely calm. I wasn't panicked about seeing Dene and I wasn't nervous about getting what I had to say to her right. Everything Michelle had said had made perfect sense. The longer I thought about it, the more I understood. I needed to apologise to Dene and to be there for her. I needed to stop judging and let her do her thing. That, and move forward like Michelle said. Easy.

On the bus I checked my phone. A post from Dene popped up, a close-up pic of her wearing a red nose—her annual tribute to her sister, Lilly. I'd seen her Red-Nose-Day posts in the past.

I miss you every day. I wonder what you'd look like, what you'd sound like, what it would feel like to hug you. I wonder about all the things we'd do together. What being a sister would've been like. But I am your sister.

I'll always be your sister. Where you are and where I am doesn't change that.

Donate generously, Dene Queens. #rednoseday #sisterlove #denequeens #walkwithmewalker #ncwalker #youngandfree #livingthedream

I stared at Dene's image, at her words. *But I am your sister. I'll always be your sister.*

I thought of the day she gave me and Maddy the bluebird rings. *We're a sisters club.*

I thought of the night she'd slept over at my house. *We're sisters. You can't break that.*

Dene had chosen me. *Me* to be her sister.

I quickly hearted the post, more sure than ever that she'd understand. What had I been so worried about? I was so stupid! I'd tell her that I got it now. Living online wasn't easy. I'd explain, she'd forgive me and things would go back to normal. We were sisters. She'd said it herself: you can't break that.

I called out to Dene as soon as I stepped off the bus. She was standing outside the main entry gate with Maddy. Dene had her back to me. She didn't turn around. I wondered if she was wearing earbuds.

'Dene!' I shouted again.

Maddy looked my way. She pulled a face, leant in close to Dene and whispered something. *Still* Dene didn't turn around.

I walked up to them. 'Hey. Can't you hear me?'

Dene turned, but she looked right through me. She waved to someone, a girl called Clarissa from Maddy's year, who bounded up to her and embraced her in a neck-hanger hug.

'Maaaaaaate!' Clarissa squealed. 'Did you hear that we're on for tonight?'

'Yes!' Dene cried. 'Can't wait!'

'What's happening tonight?' I asked.

No one answered. The girls huddled together in a tight circle.

My stomach lurched, but I decided to pretend I didn't notice. Maybe if I ignored it they'd stop? *Fake it till you make it.* Isn't that what they say?

'Dene,' I said, tapping her shoulder. 'Can I talk to you?'

Maddy's expression was a mixture of annoyance and glee. 'We're busy,' she snapped.

'Hey,' I said, poking Dene's shoulder. 'Please?'

Dene spun on her heel to face me. 'What, Tully?'

I looked at the others, my cheeks burning. *'Alone?'* I pleaded.

Dene crossed her arms. 'I think we've said all we need to say.'

She went to turn her back, but I stopped her.

'Please, Dene?'

She planted her hands on her hips. 'Do you know what day it is?'

I looked at her blankly.

'You liked my post,' she prompted.

Red Nose Day! I pulled a handful of gold coins from my pocket to show her. 'Yes! I'm going to buy a nose at lunchtime. And I'm getting one for Michelle and Luke too.'

She barely reacted. 'Good. Then you'll know I'm not really in the mood.' She turned around and went back to talking to Maddy and Clarissa.

I walked away, wounded, but I wasn't planning on giving up. When I got a chance to be alone with Dene I knew she'd talk. She'd understand. We were best friends. This was all just an act in front of the other girls.

During History, I scrolled through Dene's old posts. There were some I hadn't liked and I didn't know if it was because I'd missed them back when, or if it was because my feed hadn't properly refreshed.

Mr Khan didn't notice what I was doing. Some teachers are totally blind. He's one of them. I sat at the back of the room in the corner where I could angle my laptop away from the view of everyone. If Mr Khan approached me, I'd simply flip screens. If Harrison, who was sitting next to me, glanced my way, he wouldn't be able to see anything. Not that what I was doing mattered to him. He was busy carving a phallic symbol into the desktop with his compass. Auguste Rodin in the making.

I stifled a giggle when I found pics of Dene trying to skateboard. The first was majorly awkward, her helmet askew, hands outstretched like she was grabbing for a non-existent rail. The second was of her on her bum, legs in the air, the skateboard shooting off unmanned (or *unwomaned*). The third was of a giant bandaid on her elbow and a nasty graze down her right arm.

Sk8 d8 disaster, m8. #skatergirl #bangedup #ouchie #denequeens #walkwithmewalker #dontskatewithmewalker #ncwalker #youngandfree #livingthedream

I hearted it and moved on.

I found another batch of photos of Dene cooking cupcakes. Kaz's galley kitchen looked like someone had dumped a bag of flour from a great height, coating it white. It was all over Dene too—in her hair, on her face, blanketing her clothes. She looked pained and exhausted.

Aint no chef!! #cupcakefate #cookingsucks #bakeryfakery #orderitinstead #denequeens #walkwithmewalker

151

I hearted that post too.

During the double lesson I found about thirty posts I hadn't previously reacted to. Some, I commented, saying nice things. Dene would like that. It helps increase her circulation. Comments are powerful. If there are comments, the algorithms pick it up and they show it to more people. Dene would be happy with me.

Just as Mr Khan was wrapping up class, my phone buzzed.

Dene: Meet me on the oval

I texted a smiley face and a thumbs up. I needed to learn to trust my gut more often. I *knew* she'd be okay if I could talk to her alone.

I packed up my gear at lightning speed and dashed past Mr Khan, who quipped, 'I wonder where Cathy Freeman is off to?'

At my locker, I threw my stuff inside and slammed the door. I headed to the oval, thinking about the things Dene and I had done, the laughs we'd shared, the time we'd spent together. I knew in my heart everything would be okay. We'd argued before and made up. A friendship couldn't disappear into thin air.

I spotted her sitting on the grass, leaning against a goalpost. She was alone, earbuds in, and she didn't see me until I was up close.

I plopped down in front of her, legs crossed. 'Hey!'
I said. 'I'm so glad we finally get to talk. I know you're
angry about the other day, but I've had a big think
about it, and if you just let me expl—'

She extracted her earbuds and held up her phone.
'You've been going through my old posts.'

I nodded. 'It increases your hits.'

Her mouth was a thin line. Eyes ablaze, she said,
'You know that when you like the old stuff, the old
stuff starts recirculating? It's annoying. People have
moved on. They're not interested in the old stuff.
They're interested in *now*.' She tossed her phone face
down in the grass. 'You know what else, Tully? It's
creepy going through my old stuff. Why would you
do that?'

I was suddenly short of breath. 'Because you said
it's a business. I was trying to get on board and help
you.'

'I don't need your help,' she said. 'And I don't think
we should hang out anymore.'

My shortness of breath became a gasp. '*What are
you talking about?*'

'That's it. We're done.'

'But Dene, if you let me—'

'I've had people do this before, Tully. I've told you

that. And now here we are with you doing *exactly* the same thing.'

I stared at her. 'That's not what I was—'

'Save it.'

She started to hoist herself to her feet. I reached out and grabbed her arm, willing her to stay, for her to talk, but she flung her hand out and caught my cheek, whacking it hard.

I reeled back, my skin stinging, not believing what had just happened.

She stood up. 'Don't touch me!'

I was crying now. *Heaving.* My stomach felt like it would climb into my throat, wedge in my mouth and permanently stop me from speaking.

She turned to walk away.

I yelled out, 'My mum rang me this morning!'

She stopped, her back to me.

'Please don't do this to me today,' I sobbed. 'Not on the same day as her.'

It was a lie. A desperate lie. My mum hadn't called. But I didn't care. I'd use anything—*anything* to make Dene stay.

'She's really sick,' I said. 'She might be dying.'

Dene took a slow step forward—a step *away* from me.

I scrambled to my feet. I was sobbing now, my

whole body wracked with disbelief that I was losing her. 'Please, Dene! You said we were friends!'

She laughed. 'God, you haven't even known me that long!'

I held up my hand and pointed to my ring. '*You* said we were sisters!'

Her jaw dropped open. 'Oh my god! I can't believe you'd say that. Today. Of all the days.'

'But it's what *you* said!'

She rolled her eyes. 'People say stuff, Tully.'

'What's that supposed to mean?'

'It means it's probably true when they say it. They say stuff one day and the next day they feel something different.'

'But *you* said you were here because you want to be here.'

She shrugged. 'And now I don't.'

Her words were a sword slicing me in half.

'Don't say that.' It came out as a whisper.

'You don't own me!' Dene yelled. 'Get it, Tully? No one does!'

'Are you kidding?' I spat, anger rising up. 'The whole world owns you, Dene! That's what you get when you share everything with everyone!'

'And there it is!' she barked triumphantly. 'What this is *really* about.' She turned to walk away. 'I'd say it's been nice knowing you, but honestly? Tully Sinclair *Who?*'

I doubled over, collapsing in on myself, crying hard.

In my whole life, *nothing* would ever hurt as much as this.

Through my tears I saw her stop and pat herself down—and that's when I saw her phone still lying in the grass.

There's a moment. A pause. A gap where things can go either way.

A choice.

I chose.

I stomped on her phone. Glass shattered, crunching underfoot. *Crack. Crack. Crack.* Cracked like my heart.

I picked it up, marched up to her and rammed it at her chest. 'I hope you're happy,' I snarled, 'with all your real-life friends!'

She blinked at me, her fingers curling around her phone.

Maybe it was wishful thinking, but I swear I saw regret in her eyes.

CHAPTER SIXTEEN

#NoBigDeal

There's a very real possibility I could spend the rest of my life under my doona.

The human body needs sustenance, hydration, Vitamin D, exercise, oxygen. I could get most of those things in bed. Open the window, let the sunlight and fresh air in. Wait for Michelle to bring me food and water. Exercise? I got that every time my heart raced going over what had happened with Dene. Yep, I could stay under my doona until I sprouted grey hair, smelled like mothballs and lavender, wore slippers and got around with a Zimmer frame.

But what about the hygiene thing? Everyone needs to poo. It's as essential to living as is the rest.

Now I needed the loo. I had to leave my room.

I opened the door and stuck my head out to check if the coast was clear, and I tiptoed down the hallway.

Like some freak with extra-sensory perception, Luke emerged from the laundry, a basket of washing in his arms.

'Ah! She lives,' he said.

'Rack off, stalker.'

He gave a boisterous laugh. 'Interesting choice of words!'

'Why?'

'Because word on the street is that you're exactly that.'

I flung open the bathroom door, walked in and slammed it shut behind me, locking it. 'Get lost!' I yelled.

'It's why you're in hiding, isn't it?' It sounded like he was standing directly outside the door. 'It's why you won't show your face. You've gone full Sia on us.'

'Sia?'

'That pop star who doesn't like to show her face,' Luke said.

'People who go to the toilet generally hide from the view of others, Luke,' I said.

'You know what I'm talking about.'

My heart stung. *What were people saying about me?* I hadn't checked my phone. I couldn't bring myself to.

'Fill me in,' he said. 'What happened?'

'No. Go away!' I yelled.

'No can do,' he said, rapping his hand on the door. 'I'm fulfilling the brother–sister contract. It's my divine right to torture you.'

'It's an overused narrative!' I shouted. And then I burst into tears.

He must've heard, because he suddenly sounded gentle and sincere. 'I was just mucking around, Tully. I'm sorry. Dene's a self-absorbed princess. Forget her.'

I couldn't bring myself to answer him. Dene had hurt me, but I didn't think that about her. I found it really hard to think bad things at all. But it felt nice that (for once!) Luke was on my side.

'Not everyone believes she's all that,' Luke said. 'Lots of people have never heard of her.'

That wasn't true. Everyone at school had heard of her, even before she'd enrolled.

'I have an idea,' Luke said. 'Name me six of your favourite Hollywood actresses.'

I stared at the toilet door. 'Why?'

'Just do it. Go.'

I quickly named six. 'Margot Robbie. Charlize Theron. Saoirse Ronan. Riley Keough. Jena Malone. Jameela Jamil.'

'Good,' Luke said. 'Now name me six of your favourite influencers.'

I tried. I stopped after three. I could visualise their posts, but I couldn't think of their Insta handles, or even their names.

'See?' Luke said. 'Influencers are not the big deal you think they are.'

'*You* thought Dene was a big deal,' I argued.

'Did not.'

'Did so,' I said. 'You stuttered when you met her. You could barely string two words together.'

'I was holding in a fart,' Luke said.

I burst out laughing.

'Aaaaaaaand that's my cue to leave!' Luke said, his voice fading. 'Job done, sense of humour reinstated. Catch ya later, sis.'

He left.

And I got to sit in peace. And cry.

It's weird how you can laugh and cry at the same time. Like when Michelle hauled me out of bed on Day-I-Don't-Know-What-After-Dene-Dumped-Me and told me my self-imposed isolation was officially over. I'd been in 'the hole' too long. It was time to reintegrate with Gen-Pop.

'What's Gen-Pop?' I asked groggily, as she steered me in the direction of the shower.

'*General population* is where prison inmates

interact. They're let out of their cells and they mingle. *You* will mingle with your fellow students. You're rejoining them. You're returning to Gen-Pop.'

'What if I don't want to?' I said, taking off my T-shirt.

'Too bad.'

'You can't make me,' I whined.

'I can and I will,' she said.

In the bathroom, she reached above me, angled the showerhead, turned on the taps and pushed me under. I still had my undies on. The water hadn't had time to warm up and it was freezing.

I hugged myself, teeth chattering, jumping in circles and shrieking with shock. *'What are you doing? Are you freakin' crazy?'*

'Time to wash away the misery!' Michelle grabbed the shampoo and squirted it on my head. Goo ran into my eyes. 'You're lucky I don't shave your head,' she said. 'It would certainly be easier to deal with.'

I snatched her razor from the soap-holder and handed it to her. 'Go for it.'

'And give you another reason to not go to school? Forget it.'

That's when I started cry-laughing. *'I'm never going to school again! Ever! Ever! Ever!'*

Michelle pressed her lips. She gave me a don't-pull-this-crap shake of her head. 'You've got to get it together, Tully. This isn't healthy.'

'*Can you please leave?*'

She closed the shower door. The water had finally turned warm and was steaming up the glass. I kicked off my undies and washed my hair.

'I'll sit here until you're done,' Michelle said, parking her bum on the side of the bath. 'Tell me what you'd like in your lunchbox. I have smiley-face luncheon meat. Do you want that with sauce?'

She really was going to make me go to school. There was no way I was getting out of it.

Still, I tried. 'Please, Michelle. It's too soon. I need a bit longer.'

'I wonder why they don't make frown-face meats?' she mused. 'They could do the whole range of emojis. What a wasted opportunity.'

'*I don't want meat in my sandwich!*' I yelled.

'What *do* you want?'

'I want my friend back!' As I let it out, my stomach clenched with an unbearable pain. I sank to the shower floor and watched water spin down the drain. 'I want my friend back,' I said over and over again, staring into the drain like it was some kind of wishing well.

Michelle opened the door. I was so upset I didn't even care that she saw me naked.

'Dene is *not* a true friend, Tully,' Michelle said.

I looked up at her. 'How do *you* know?'

'Because making you suffer like this is cruel.'

Michelle didn't know I'd smashed Dene's phone. Maybe I *did* deserve it?

She reached in, turned off the taps and put out her hand to help me. 'Come on. Let's get you dry and dressed.' She held out a towel. I stepped into it and she wrapped me in a tight hug. 'You're stronger than you think, Tully. You were fine before Dene came along and you'll be fine after.'

'Are you fine without Dad around?'

She pushed back my wet hair and searched my eyes. 'Truth?'

I nodded.

'Not in the beginning,' she said. 'It hurt every single day. But it got easier over time. Time, I've come to learn, is the only thing that makes a difference.' She spun me around, patted my bum, and walked me to my room. 'We find ways to cope, Tully. We find other loves to make up for those we lose.'

I turned to look at her. 'You really think?'

'Yes, I do. Like you, for example. I love you. You and your brother. You kids get me through.'

She winked and closed the door.
I felt a glimmer of hope.
Would I find other loves too?

CHAPTER SEVENTEEN

#LoveHate

I took off my bluebird ring. I imagined what a movie character might do and I pictured a girl standing on top of a bridge, wind whipping her hair, mascara staining her tear-streaked cheeks; I imagined her ripping off the ring and hurling it into a raging river before dusting her hands and walking away.

That girl on the bridge wasn't me. I couldn't bear to part with the ring, not yet, so I put it in my jewellery box and closed the lid—closing it like I was closing a door in my heart.

I packed my schoolbag, took my phone off its charger, held my breath and checked my notifications. Dene had posted on Insta. I desperately wanted to ignore it, to unfollow, delete, block, redirect, send it to Saturn and Neptune via twenty loops around the sun. But I couldn't resist the urge. I opened it.

It was another endorsement post, this time for stationery products. In some ways that was easier to take. Had it been about Maddy or another friend, it would've hurt more.

In the photo, pretty pink flowers decorated a large notepad embossed with Dene's name. Dene was in the background, a pen between her teeth, her expression contemplative.

Do you have something you want to say to someone special but you don't know how to say it? #writersblock #myveryownstationery #getyours #denequeens #walkwithmewalker #ncwalker #youngandfree #livingthedream

My heart raced. Was she talking about me? Was *I* that someone special and this was her way of telling me?

What would happen if she came running up to me, apologetic, wanting me back? Would I give in? How could I after what she'd done to me?

Now I knew *exactly* what people meant when they said they love-hated someone. I love-hated Dene so much right now.

And I hated feeling that way.

First lesson was Art. I was relieved to see Kira sitting

by the window and I made a beeline for the stool next to her. She was busy hauling her sketchbook from her bag. She didn't exactly whoop with joy when she saw me.

'Hey,' she said stiffly.

'Hi,' I said, sitting down and getting my things out.

After a few awkward moments she said, 'I thought you must have forgotten what I look like.'

I dry-swallowed.

'*And* lost my number,' she added.

'That's not true,' I said meekly.

She crossed her arms. 'It *is* true. You only remember me when you want something, Tully.'

I wanted to argue, to make excuses, but I didn't have any. Kira was right.

She looked me over. 'Do you know that whenever we talk—which is like *not at all* lately—you never ask me what's going on in my life. It's always about you.'

I tried to think of her recent posts—of family photos, or the things she'd been doing outside of school—but I couldn't recall any of it. I didn't have a clue what was going on in her world.

'You're right,' I said, genuinely ashamed.

'You forgot my birthday,' Kira said.

I cowered, knowing *exactly* how I'd felt when I thought Dene had done that to me. 'Kira, I'm so sorry!'

'*You're sorry?*' Her eyes welled with tears. '*Sorry!* Is that all you can say? You made me feel like I'm nothing! A nobody! Just some total random you talk to now and then. Totally worthless!'

'That's not true.'

'It *is* true! It's true to me! It's how *you* made *me* feel!'

'I didn't realise I—'

'You don't realise a lot of things, Tully. You're too busy thinking about yourself.'

Her lips were a thin line. She looked me up and down, shaking her head.

'You're *not* worthless...' I said feebly. 'Not to me, you're not.'

'Yeah?' Kira huffed, wiping her eyes. 'You have a strange way of showing it.'

She was right. She was totally right.

I picked up my stuff. 'It's probably best if I move.' I slid off the stool. 'I know it means nothing to you, Kira,' I said, looking straight into her eyes, 'but I *am* sorry. More sorry than you'll ever know.' I really meant it too. I'd screwed up in a massive way. I was a crap person and I was owning it.

I turned to go, but she put her hand on my arm. 'Wait,' she said.

Her expression softened and she pulled my

sketchbook towards her. Our homework had been to draw a silhouette. I'd done one of myself, side-on, my hair in a ponytail, shirt collar turned up. I wasn't sure if we were supposed to draw someone more recognisable, like a famous person or something, because as usual I'd been distracted when the instruction was given, thinking about Dene. I hoped I'd got it right.

Kira ran her hands over the paper. 'This is really good. Did you spray fixative over the pastels?'

I felt grateful not only for her positive feedback, but because she was being kind to me. She could've easily chosen never to speak to me again.

'Yes,' I said, sitting back on the stool. 'I was going to do a watercolour, but I thought pastels would give it pop.'

'It's wonderful,' she said, tapping the page. She flipped open her sketchbook and showed me hers, a silhouette of a horse. It was incredible.

'Jeepers!' I breathed. 'Acrylic?'

Kira nodded, obviously proud. 'Can you see the blues meshed with the black?'

'Yes,' I said eagerly. 'And tiny flicks of hot pink too. And Kira! The proportion, the way you have it positioned on the page, the motion…It's brilliant!'

She beamed. 'Thank you.'

We smiled at each other and it felt good. Like

something lost had been found.

'I'm really sorry, Kira. I stuffed up in a big way.'

I meant it—I truly did. There was much more I could've said, but I didn't know how to make the words come out right. Could they ever be enough to make up for what I'd done?

Kira was going to say something, when Ms Brian opened the classroom door. Students started streaming in. There were some not-so-familiar faces, which meant we must be having another joint class—and *that* meant Dene would be walking in any moment.

I frantically looked around. The chairs next to us were taken, thank goodness. I knew I was being a pathetic spineless loser, but I couldn't help it. The idea of being anywhere near Dene hurt too much.

Kira's hand closed over mine. Until she touched me, I didn't realise I'd been shaking.

There was warmth in her eyes. 'It's okay,' she whispered.

Relief washed over me—*and* a terrible sick feeling. I didn't deserve Kira. I'd been a terrible friend. I'd blown her off multiple times. If she'd completely snubbed me, I'd get it. I'd one thousand per cent get it. I didn't deserve to have a friend in the world.

'I've heard some stuff,' Kira whispered. 'I know you, Tully, and I know it's not true.'

'Heard what?' I was terrified of the answer.

She shook her head. 'Doesn't matter. What I know is this: you would've felt with your heart first and thought with your head later. You're that kind of person.'

Tears clouded my eyes. I couldn't speak.

Kira said, 'It's been like a car crash in slow-mo.' As usual, she wasn't mincing words. 'I wondered where it would end.'

That car crash walked in.

Dene was the driver; I was the passenger. Or I was the driver and *she* the passenger. I didn't know anymore. Maybe we were both in the back seat with no one at the wheel.

Dene didn't scan the room looking for anyone. She didn't seem particularly interested in who was there. She definitely wasn't looking for me. She found a seat, pulled out her phone and kept her head down.

Kira's hand remained wrapped around mine. 'I'm here,' she said.

I smiled and nodded. 'Thank you. For everything.'

'I know, I know,' Kira said with a wink. 'I'm a freakin' wonderful friend. You don't have to tell me.'

I shoved her sideways. She shoved me back, giggling.

Out of the corner of my eye I saw Dene look up at us.

She *was* watching.

I slung my arm around Kira and pressed my cheek to hers. Kira scruffed my hair. I pinched her nose. We laughed. The message was clear: *We were close. We were mates. We were strong. I wasn't alone.*

And yet I knew what I was doing—I was using Kira. I was a horrible despicable person—a *desperate person*. But if there was a small chance Dene would see us and be jealous, that watching us have fun together would change her mind, I had to try.

I surreptitiously looked Dene's way and saw her fiddling with her phone again. Her expression was unreadable. I wanted her to be annoyed. Or sad. Uncomfortable. *Something.* She didn't show any emotion. She sat there seemingly bulletproof. Maybe you are when you live so much of your life in the public eye.

Except I knew that wasn't the truth. She hurt just like I did.

Ms Brian circled the room, critiquing our work. She gave me and Kira high praise for our silhouettes. Ms Brian said that Dene's drawing of author Virginia Woolf showed initiative and insight beyond her years. She held it up for the class to admire. Harrison commented that Virginia had a big nose and this prompted Ms Brian to launch into an epic monologue on Virginia's literary-goddess status. Most of the class zoned out. Dene was clearly embarrassed she'd provoked such a discussion. That gave me a sense of justice. Dene was suffering. And *again* I was a horrible despicable person.

After class, Kira walked with me to the lockers. 'I have PE now,' she said. 'You?'

I checked my timetable. 'Maths.'

'Meet you at lunch?' Kira asked.

I couldn't hide my relief. 'That'd be awesome.'

'Cool, see you then.' She walked off, with a bounce in her step.

I was digging around for my calculator when I felt someone standing behind me.

'Have you still got it?' came Dene's voice.

I turned around. I had no idea what she was talking about.

'The bluebird ring,' she said. 'I want it back.'

My gaze darted to her hand. She was still wearing hers. *Why was she still wearing hers?*

'I want to give it to someone else,' she said. A smirk edged her lips. 'Leave it at the front office in an envelope addressed to me.'

She walked off.

That's when I went home.

~

Michelle opened the door, blinking with surprise. 'Tully?'

I shoved past her, straight to my bedroom.

'Tully!' she called, anger tinging her voice. 'What are you doing home?'

'I hate you!' I shouted. 'Why'd you make me go to school? *Why?*'

I reached my room and slammed the door. I grabbed my desk chair, jammed it under the doorknob and sat down just as Michelle tried to open the door.

She managed to get it open a tiny bit. 'Tully! Oh for heaven's sake! Move out of the way!'

'No!'

She thumped the door. 'Move!'

'No!'

She stopped, and in a gentler voice she said, 'We don't speak to each other like this, Tully. We don't—'

'I know!' I screamed. 'We hold civilised conversations! We use our words! We express our grievances in an appropriate tone and manner! I don't care! Do you understand? I! Don't! Care!'

'What happened?'

'What do you *think* happened?'

She didn't say anything for a moment. Then she announced, 'Right. It's time for me to call Kaz. If Dene is bullying you, I'm going to put a stop to it.'

I jumped off the chair, pushed it aside and opened the door. 'No! Please, Michelle! Don't do that!'

She raised her eyebrows at me. 'Why not?'

Because deep down I knew it wasn't *all* Dene's fault—it was mine too. But I didn't know how to explain any of that, so instead I said, 'Because if you do that she'll never speak to me again!'

'I thought that was the present state of affairs anyway!'

'You don't understand. Just go away.' I tried to push the door but Michelle pressed her hand flat against it, holding it open.

'Tully, you can't keep this up. Dene said it's over, so it's over! Boundaries, hon. You have to respect other people's boundaries. You can't spend your life on hold waiting for her to come back.'

'Why not?' I yelled. 'It's what you do with Dad!'

It was as if I'd shot her. Michelle looked stunned for a moment, then turned and hobbled down the hallway. I followed her, my heart pounding, head swimming. I couldn't accept any of this was really happening.

Michelle grabbed her mobile from the dining table and started hitting buttons. I jumped at her, trying to snatch it, but she ducked out of the way, wincing in pain as she did and clutching her back.

I heard Dad's voice on loudspeaker. 'Michelle,' he said, 'I'm in a meeting right now. Can I call you back?'

Not, *Hi, how are you going?* Not, *Hi, it's nice to hear from you.* Not, *Is it important?*

'No, you can't,' Michelle said stiffly. 'It's urgent.'

'Michelle, I'm busy right now—'

'It's about Tully,' she interrupted, looking directly at me. There were tears in her eyes.

'Okay, but can it wait half an hour?' Dad asked.

'It's important!'

'What's happened?' There was a sudden waver in Dad's voice. 'Is she hurt?'

'No,' Michelle said. 'Not exactly.'

His concern dissolved. 'Then it's not life-threateningly urgent, is it?'

'She's upset,' Michelle said.

'She's a teenage girl,' Dad said. 'They're always upset.'

I froze. *What did he just say?*

'This is different,' Michelle pleaded. 'I'm really worried about her.'

Dad chuckled. 'I'm sure it's nothing. She's just being dramatic. Trust me, in a week or two she'll be upset about something else.'

'No,' Michelle said. 'You need to come home.'

Dad's voice became a strangled hiss. 'Michelle,

we've had this conversation before. I'm *trying* to make a go of it here. You know that. That was the deal.'

'Your kids need you,' Michelle interrupted. 'Tully needs you *right now.*'

There was a long pause. Dad sighed. 'Look, I'll call her tonight. But I genuinely don't have the time right now. I'm under the pump as it is.'

'Do you even want to know what it's about?' Michelle asked.

He didn't answer.

Michelle took a deep breath. 'Tully had a falling out with her best friend. She's heartbroken and she doesn't want to go to school.'

Dad laughed. *He actually laughed.* 'Right. Okay. Like I said I'll call her tonight, okay?'

He hung up.

Michelle put the phone on the table. I stared at it, choking back tears.

'I'm sorry I had to do that,' Michelle said. 'But some people aren't ready, Tully, no matter how hard you try. They're not ready until they decide to be ready.'

I walked around to her side of the table and fell into her arms, crying and hugging her tight.

'It's okay,' she whispered, stroking my hair. 'It'll be okay.'

Dad called at nine o'clock when Michelle and I were watching an old movie called *Love Actually*. We'd only just started it when I saw my phone flashing on the coffee table. I reached over and hit Decline.

Michelle smiled. She passed me the popcorn. 'Boundaries,' she said. 'People set theirs. It's time you set yours.'

I pulled the throw rug over my lap and snuggled into her.

CHAPTER EIGHTEEN

#Enough

Love Actually is a really cool film. I actually loved it—which is possibly how it got its name. There are heaps of characters and their lives all overlap, and I loved keeping track of all of the connections. There are lots of funny bits too. Like the old rocker dude. He's a crack-up. And the actor who plays Professor Snape in Harry Potter is in it.

Michelle said *Love Actually* is an entertaining story, but she thinks it contains some screwed-up messages. I'm like, *What messages?* And she talked about the bit where the guy who's in love with Keira Knightley's character stands on her doorstep holding placards, telling her he loves her, while her partner is watching TV inside their apartment. I thought that was romantic, but Michelle said it was a warped male perspective, his actions were creepy and he needed to learn that No means No.

I wasn't a hundred per cent sure about all that and I wondered if she was reading too much into it. But it gave me an idea. I know Michelle said I needed to set boundaries, but *Love Actually* made me think that fighting for the person you care about is important too. Maybe I didn't fight hard enough for Dene. Maybe I owed it to her *and* to myself to give it one last try.

I dug out my old Science posters from under my bed, the ones I'd done on stiff coloured cardboard, and turned them over. They were blank on the back. Perfect.

I got to work, writing my message in thick black texta, taking ages to get the block capital letters right, colouring them thick and dark. When I was finished, I put the posters on my desk and I stood back to get a good view. They were awesome, without a doubt. There was no way this was the product of a warped male perspective. I was a girl. Dene was a girl. This was about friendship.

The more I thought about it, the more I thought it was a brilliant idea. If someone did this for me I'd feel pretty happy. If a person went to all this effort it would mean they truly cared about me. And I *did* truly care about Dene.

Before going to bed I saw an Insta meme that said *To err is human, to forgive is divine.*

The girl who posted it said that forgiving people and moving on was good for them, but it was *also* good for you because you got to let go of all the sadness in your heart. She'd posted lots of smiley faces and lovehearts all over it. It had a really happy vibe. I felt like it was a sign, as if I was meant to stumble across the meme. The universe was sending me a secret message.

I rolled the posters up and put them in my back-pack, and I told Michelle I was going for a walk. She said fresh air was a great idea. I'd worked out the bus route to Dene's house. I had to take three buses, but I could get there by four-thirty. Dene would likely be doing her homework.

On the bus, I wondered if I should ring the doorbell when I got there. In *Love Actually*, the guy is lucky when Keira Knightley's character opens the door. It could've been her partner who answered, but it wasn't. The loved-up dude holds up a sign that tells Keira to say it's carol singers.

What if Kaz opened the door? What would I say? Did she even know that Dene and I weren't speaking? What if Dene answered? I couldn't really tell her that it was carol singers. It wasn't anywhere near Christmas.

I thought that standing on the lawn and throwing

something at Dene's window to get her attention was the best idea. But what if Dene wasn't in her room? What if she was in the kitchen making a snack? What would happen then? Did the scriptwriters think through this stuff when they wrote the movie? The Keira Knightley character could've been on the toilet when the dude rang the doorbell. She might've been waxing her top lip. She could've stubbed her toe on the way down the hallway and be wailing like a banshee when she opened the door.

Why isn't life like it is in books and movies?

By the time I reached Dene's house, I was shaking with adrenaline. This was it. This was my big moment. This was the scene where I was going to make her see sense.

I stood in her driveway and looked up at her window. To my surprise, she was sitting at her desk, hunched over some books and eating an apple. (Okay, so maybe life *was* going to imitate art. Go figure.) I briefly thought of the personalised stationery she'd posted on Insta and wondered if she was writing a letter to me.

I jumped up and down in the driveway, waving my arms around. Sure enough, she looked down at me—and her expression was like she couldn't believe what she saw.

I whipped out my posters and put them on the ground, colour-coded in a specific order. Green was first.

I'M SORRY I SAID THE WRONG THING

I put that down. Red next.

I DIDN'T MEAN TO HURT YOU

Dene was now leant across her desk, her face close to the window.

Yellow.

YOU'RE THE BEST FRIEND EVER. I MISS YOU

Finally blue.

IT'S NOT XMAS, BUT MY WISH
IS THAT YOU'D COME BACK

I put it down, threw my arms in the air and with a huge smile, took a bow. I did a curtsy too, to cover all bases.

When I looked up again, Dene was gone. Was she on her way downstairs to meet me? I rolled up the posters and put them in my bag.

The front door opened. It was Kaz.

'Tully,' she said with a delighted tone. There was a phone in her hand, pressed to her chest as if I'd interrupted a call. 'Could you sit on the bench over there?' She pointed to a concrete seat nestled in the garden bed. 'Dene will be out soon.'

My heart leapt. 'Yes!' I eagerly agreed. 'Of course!' I made my way over to the bench. 'Here?'

Kaz watched. 'Yes, that's it. Good girl. Now, just wait there, okay?'

As she closed the door she resumed her call. I heard her say something like, 'Yes, thank you, please hurry.'

I waited.

And I waited.

I brushed my hair with my hands and tucked it behind my ears. I checked my reflection using the camera selfie function. I looked good—no puffy eyes, no red face. I smiled and checked my teeth. No seeds stuck in there, no spinach. (When was the last time I ate spinach? I wasn't sure.) I blew on my hand and smelled my breath. Not bad. I got a mint chewy from my bag and munched on it just to be safe. I spat it into the grass. I pulled out my lip gloss and put some on. I crossed and uncrossed my legs, sat facing forward, sidesaddle, straddling the bench, stood up, a foot on the seat, elbow on my knee and hand under my chin. I sat down again. I tugged my clothes straight and smooth. I picked off pieces of fluff and flicked them away and checked the time. I wasn't sure how long I'd been waiting. Maybe fifteen minutes? Perhaps Dene had gone to the bathroom to make herself look nice. Maybe she was putting on make-up. Maybe she'd received an unexpected phone call and she was busy with that.

I heard the purr of a car engine. Gravel crunched as the vehicle turned into Dene's U-shaped driveway. *Not now! Don't be some delivery driver and ruin my big moment!*

A car door opened and closed.

I turned around. It was Michelle.

She stared at me, then at the house. I followed her gaze and I saw Kaz and Dene at Dene's bedroom window, looking down at us. Kaz had her arm wrapped protectively around Dene.

Michelle extended her hand for me. She said quietly, 'Come on, sweetheart. Come with me.'

I stood up and slowly walked towards her, each step heavier than the last. My heart felt like it was crumbling into a million pieces.

I climbed into the car and put my bag by my feet.

'Enough now,' Michelle said, pulling out of the driveway. 'Enough.'

CHAPTER NINETEEN

#LoseYourself

Michelle let me stay home again. I *was* sick this time. I'd come down with some flu-type virus. Michelle said that that's what happens when you get run-down: your immune system gives up on you. She said it was probably a mistake to force me to go to school and that mental-health days are just as important as sick days—and I was in need of both. She gave me two Panadol.

She encouraged me to sit at the table and draw. *Art therapy*, she called it. She got out the easel she'd given me for my birthday and spread all my paints, pastels and pencils around me, plus a few books for inspiration. She put a bowl of salt-and-vinegar chips on one side of the table, and a bowl of Haighs hundreds-and-thousands chocolate buttons on the other. Also a box of tissues.

She patted my shoulder and whispered, 'Lose your-self, darling.'

I thought she'd told me *not* to lose myself.

But I sucked it up and did as she said. I drew. I didn't know what else to do anyway. I thought of Mum and wondered if this was why she made art. For the distraction, the solitude; because of all the things that overwhelmed her. Because you can be in control of your own little world.

Huh? I probably *was* my mother.

I lost track of time. I sat there drawing for hours, stopping only to go to the toilet or to blow my nose. Michelle worked on her laptop, tap tap tapping away. I had no idea what she was doing. I didn't ask. Every so often she'd get up and boil the kettle and pour me another cup of tea with lemon and honey. *Boost your immune system! Help fight the bad guys!*

The bad guy I was fighting was me.

Why was I so stupid? What did I think I'd achieve by going to Dene's house? I'd made an embarrassment of myself. It wouldn't surprise me if Dene had posted about me and told the whole world what a crazed maniac stalker I was. She'd already blocked me on all her socials. There was no way I could check—not unless I asked Michelle or Luke, and I wasn't going to do that. I thought about messaging Kira and asking her, but that idea made me cringe.

Wow. I really *was* thinking like a stalker. *Stop thinking, Tully! Just do!*

I kept working, trying hard all the while not to let my head wander. Eventually I'd completed five drawings: a series of black and white sketches using charcoal pencil and fine-tip black pen. I guess you could say they were Escher inspired, featuring humanoid figurines, twisting roads and bridges, staircases and rolling landscapes. I'd tried to use the charcoal and black pen to provide depth and perspective.

I visited the Escher Museum in the Netherlands when I was six years old. It was on Mum and Dad's 'save the marriage' European holiday—not that I knew that's what it was; Dad only told me afterwards. Mum wanted to see *all* the galleries and *all* the museums. My memory is hazy, but I remember a room at the Escher Museum that had a black-and-white checkered floor. When you stood against the wall in one corner you looked enormous, and when someone stood in the other corner, they looked tiny. We laughed our heads off because I looked taller than Dad.

That's what Escher did—he played with perspective. He used a trick of the eye. He harnessed the idea that the mind sees what it expects to see.

Michelle gave my sketches a solid once-over. 'Gosh Tully! These are really wonderful!' she said.

'You think?' I said miserably. 'I think they're crap.'

It was true. I couldn't see anything positive. Only faults. The bits that I'd shaded too heavily, where I hadn't got the balance right. It looked like a dumpster fire.

'Nonsense!' Michelle said, rubbing my head affectionately. 'I think you've outdone yourself! This one is very clever,' she said, picking up the split view of a hillside and a lake. She turned it this way and that. 'It doesn't matter which way you look at it, it's like it's saying the same thing.'

I'd patterned the hillside and lake to look similar: the wavy water and the vegetation. I was thinking of me and Dene—a kind of reflection of each other, the same but different. I also thought of us split in two, a line now between us—a line I couldn't cross.

'You should post these,' Michelle said. 'Go on. Take some pics, put them up. They're really good.'

I shrugged. 'I don't post stuff like this.'

'But your art post received so much attention!' Michelle argued.

'Because it was a picture of Dene.'

Michelle shook her head. 'You don't know that. Maybe people liked it for what it was: a fine portrait.'

I saw the eagerness in her eyes and sighed, defeated. 'Okay. I'll do it.'

If anything, maybe it would shut her up. And if I got no traction, if no one cared, it would give me a reason to hate myself all over again.

I took my pictures to the window where the light was bright and lay them on the floor. I snapped a bunch of photos from various angles, using different filters. I spent a while thinking about how to title my post and eventually I came up with 'It all depends on how you look at things'. Then I pasted a bunch of art hashtags in the comments section.

Within minutes my phone was pinging.

Michelle smirked. 'That sounds positive.'

There were a whole pile of likes from people I didn't even know. Actual followers. And my notifications told me Michelle had already commented: Wow! What an undiscovered talent. This girl is incredible! She should be famous!

I shook my head. 'Michelle...'

She blinked innocently. 'What?'

'You're my stepmother. That's cheating.'

'Not cheating,' she said with a defiant pout. 'Nepotism.'

'What?'

'When you give unfair advantage to a family

member or close friend,' she explained.

'Well it's nepotism then,' I said.

'Yes,' she said. 'But no one knows that.'

She was right. She was Michelle *Warner*, not Michelle *Sinclair*.

I smirked. 'I thought you didn't believe in selling your kids online?'

'I wouldn't call it selling,' she said. 'More *supporting*.'

'Semantics.'

Michelle laughed. 'My word-nerd tutorials are paying off!'

I couldn't contain a little grin even though I was still feeling miserable.

Another message pinged. This is unreal! I can't believe how good this is!

It was Luke.

He was on my side too.

CHAPTER TWENTY

#MyThing

By the next evening thirty-eight thousand people had liked my post.

Thirty-eight thousand!

I couldn't believe it. I thought it was a glitch. And the number kept going up.

There were heaps of comments—people wanting me to post more. I felt a rush of confidence when I read through their kind words.

@youbeaututes Can you turn this into wallpaper?

@dogbogfog Wow. And you're still at school? This is so good.

@heatseeker I can't heart this enough

@borderlineborderline You're up there with the true artistic greats!

@lastround I'm going to tell all my friends to follow you. I'll include you in my story and repost. You're brilliant!

A euphoric sparkle-cloud floated inside me. It reminded me of grade three when I'd won a sprinting race on sports day. Everyone crowded around me at the finish line, cheering and telling me what a great job I'd done. I was successful. I was worth something.

But just like on that day, another feeling lurked—*a bad one*—one I didn't really want to focus on. The bad feeling eventually came and sat next to the happy feeling, and it gradually shoved the happy feeling aside until I was left with nothing but a queasiness in my gut, a headache, and a dull pain in my chest. It said, *You can't do it again, can you?*

I wondered if this was what Dene went through each time she posted? I wished I could ask her.

Luke seemed genuinely impressed by my efforts. He posted on Facebook and linked it to my Instagram. *Check out my sis. She's talented, right?* After he did that, I ended up with even more followers and likes.

'Don't get a big head or anything,' he said.

I was at the kitchen table drawing spinning planets, shooting stars, sunbeams and refracted light. Lots of blues and yellows.

Luke flicked the switch to boil the kettle. He was making his nightly hot-chocolate concoction, which was probably just as Insta-worthy as anything I created: an old-fashioned milkshake glass, a stripy enviro-friendly metal straw, whipped cream, syrup, a banana and chocolate flakes.

'Remember I want a cut of your earnings,' he said.

'A cut?'

'Twenty per cent is fair.'

I turned out my empty jean pockets. 'You're welcome to twenty per cent of this.'

He opened a packet of Oreos. 'My marketing fee is also included,' he said. 'I'll put it all in the monthly statement.'

I laughed. 'You sound like Dad.'

'Easy there, Tiger,' Luke warned. 'Play nice. You know that *I* haven't drawn the obvious comparison.'

He was talking about Mum.

I took my chances. 'Do you think about her?'

'Of course,' he said, popping an Oreo on his tongue. He chewed, crumbs flying. 'I regularly imagine her taking a long walk off a short jetty.'

Like I said: *Anger-management issues.*

'Do you think she'll come back?' I asked.

'From the jetty?'

'Be serious.'

'I don't think so,' he said.

Luke and I rarely talked about Mum. It was sort of a mutual agreement, a silent understanding—don't bring her up, don't take off that bandage. Don't expose that wound, but here I was wanting to talk about her. I needed to—with someone who understood.

'How does it make you feel?' I asked.

He scoffed another Oreo. 'That she left? Pretty crap.'

I nodded. 'Me too.'

He looked at the ceiling. 'What was it you called it the other day? An overused narrative.'

'Huh?'

'The missing mum thing,' he said. 'Central to so many storybook characters. That makes us the heroes of the story.'

'It does?'

'Yep,' he said. 'You know the stuff that made her the way she is, right?'

I didn't know what he was talking about. 'What stuff?'

'Her family,' Luke said. 'She didn't have the best relationship with them.'

We hardly ever talked about Mum's side of the family. We didn't know them—at least not in person. Mum ran away from home when she was fifteen. Her parents, my grandparents, never spoke to her again. They died in a car crash when she was in her mid-twenties and I never got to meet them. Mum didn't go to the funeral and that's when her sister,

Aunt Laura, stopped talking to her too. Other than Aunt Laura, there's Dwayne, the creepy uncle, but we rarely see him either.

'You think her family is why she's not a good mum?' I asked.

Luke shrugged. 'Dunno. It's the best reason I can think of.'

'What about her art?' I asked.

'What about it?'

'Maybe there wasn't room for anything else?'

He shook his head. 'There's room, Tully. Look around you. Plenty of people have room for family and careers.'

Dad didn't seem to. And Dene didn't seem to either. Michelle did, but I knew it was hard for her.

'It's an excuse,' Luke said. 'If you ask me, there's not a lot of point to working your butt off and being good at something if there's no one around to share it with. Money, certificates, awards, trophies—none of it hugs you or looks after you. None of it is there for you when stuff goes wrong and you need help.'

I smiled. 'Like you look after me?'

He nodded. 'It's in the brother–sister contract.'

'I think I need to get a copy of this contract and read the fine print.'

'No need,' he said confidently. 'The bold print is

the part where I annoy you. The fine print is the part where I'm occasionally a good guy.'

'You're weird,' I said.

'You're weirder,' he said.

Michelle walked in, carrying her laptop. 'What's happening here?'

Luke held up his creamy-chocolate masterpiece. 'A sickeningly sweet conversation,' he said.

Michelle looked from Luke to me and back again. 'Right…?'

'About sibling love and family loyalties,' I added, 'which has thankfully ended.' I held up my drawing and showed them. 'What do think about this one?'

Luke gave me two thumbs up. Michelle put up both hands, wiggling ten fingers.

I took a pic and put it on Insta. Within moments my phone was pinging.

'Dene had better watch out,' Luke said with a sly smile. 'She has competition.'

I shook my head. I knew he was trying to be nice, but for the first time in a long time I didn't want to think about Dene. Not everything I did had to be about her.

'It's not a competition,' I said. 'I'm just doing my thing.'

'Good for you,' Michelle said.

I grinned.

Me.

My thing.

Mine.

(Shared publicly with thousands of strangers.)

CHAPTER TWENTY-ONE

#Bacon&Cheese

Just when you think things are getting better, they turn to crap. I posted a drawing of a magpie and a grand total of six people liked it.

Six.

'I don't understand,' I said to Kira.

It was lunchtime and we were sitting on the grass under a gum tree on the edge of the school oval, watching year-twelve girls play footy. One of them, a tall girl, kept taking all the marks. Kira had been a bit weird with me for standing her up the day I left school early, but she'd obviously decided to let it go; she was acting normal.

'All my other posts got heaps of attention. Why not this one?' I pulled up the photo and showed it to Kira. 'Is there something wrong with it?'

Kira grabbed my phone and looked closely at the

picture, scrutinising it as if something might reveal itself. 'Nope,' she said, handing it back. 'Looks good to me.'

'Then why did no one like it?'

'Social media is weird like that,' she said. 'One day it shows your stuff to everyone, and the next day it takes a holiday. It's not exactly reliable. You know what I *also* think?'

'What?'

'I think they like to mess with you.'

'They?' I said. 'They who?'

'Program designers,' Kira explained. 'App developers. In addition to being mega-smart super-geeks, I believe they're also closet psychos. They know users get excited about getting likes, so sometimes they hold them back to be mean.'

The idea surprised me. 'Is that for real?'

She shrugged. 'I don't know, but it's a possibility.'

I put down my phone. 'Hang on. So you think there's a bunch of computer wizards out there taking twisted joy in our misery?'

She nodded. 'Totally.'

I laughed. 'Conspiracy theory much?'

Kira nodded. 'Perhaps. But they know more about you than you think they do. Have you ever done the bacon test?'

'The what?'

She picked up my phone. 'I don't know what anyone else calls it, but I call it the bacon test. Watch this.' She held my phone an inch from her mouth and spoke loudly. 'Bacon, bacon, bacon, bacon, bacon, bacon, bacon. I want bacon!' She gave my phone back. 'Just you watch,' she said. 'When the bell goes, check your newsfeed.'

I went to open the screen, but she put her hand over mine, stopping me. 'Uh-uh. Not yet. No bacon deluxe for you.'

I pouted. 'I only want it if it comes with extra cheese.'

Kira whipped out her phone and turned the camera to selfie. We huddled together, chiming, 'Cheeeeeeeeese!'

She whacked the photo online, tagging me. I watched her, thinking of Dene and all the times she'd taken photos of us, never to post them. Kira did it happily. It was like our friendship was out in the open—as open as the school oval with the blue sky and the wind in our hair. With Dene I'd felt like an embarrassing secret.

Kira nudged me. 'Hey you. Where'd you go?'

I looked at her, confused. 'I'm right here.'

She tapped my forehead. 'I saw it in your eyes,

Tully. You went somewhere.'

'Oh,' I mumbled, looking away. 'It's nothing.'

'You were thinking about Dene, weren't you?' Her voice held no judgment, no annoyance. Just resignation.

'Sorry,' I said, guilt flooding me.

She patted my arm. 'It's fine. She was your friend. You genuinely liked her. I get it.' Then she added with a smirk, 'Even if I can't see what the big deal was.'

'Can I tell you a secret?' I asked nervously.

'Of course,' Kira said. 'You can tell me anything.'

I bit my lip.

'*Anything*,' she repeated.

I looked at the girls playing footy. The tall girl had taken another mark in front of the goals. She was lining up, ready to kick.

'Sometimes I get so upset about what happened, I think about doing something bad.'

Kira frowned. 'You mean to Dene?'

I shook my head.

The tall girl missed. She crouched down, slumped over, head in her hands. Then she thumped the ground with her fist—*hard*. I recognised her anger. I knew exactly what it felt like.

Kira asked, 'Do you mean you want to hurt yourself?'

I nodded.

She drew a sharp breath. 'Why would you want to do that?'

I felt tears coming. I tried to look at her, but I couldn't. 'Sometimes I think that if something bad happened to me, it would make the people I care about care about *me* again.'

'Oh Tully,' Kira sighed. 'You mean like if you ended up in hospital or something?'

I nodded, ashamed.

Kira uncrossed her legs and lay back in the grass, staring up at the trees. I did the same. We lay side by side, a ceiling of blue sky and rustling green leaves above us.

'That happened to my mum,' Kira said.

'What do you mean?'

Kira rolled onto her side to look at me. 'Mum didn't do it intentionally. She got sick. She had appendicitis and she was admitted to hospital. But a week before that happened, her friend Annie who she'd been friends with her whole life—for thirty-five years, in fact—dumped her. They had this massive fight and Annie told Mum she never wanted to speak to her again. Mum was devastated. I remember her walking around the house, crying non-stop. She got so angry, she smashed a few photo frames that held pictures of them together. Anyway, when Mum was in hospital, she said she thought Annie would see sense; she thought Annie would put their differences aside and call and check if she was okay.'

'And did she?'

Kira shook her head. 'They had a mutual friend, Kelly, who rang Annie and told her that Mum was in hospital. Kelly said it was serious and that Mum might die. Annie acted like she couldn't care less. She never picked up the phone, never sent flowers or a card, never bothered to follow up and see if Mum was okay.'

I couldn't believe it. 'That's terrible! And after they'd been friends for so long!'

'Yep,' Kira agreed. 'And that's when Mum realised that they truly weren't good for each other anymore. They might've been once, but that time was over.'

We lay there a while, not speaking, watching the clouds poking between the tree branches.

Eventually I said, 'Don't you think it sucks, Kira, how two people can be close, but it takes only one of them to change their mind? What happens to the person who *didn't* change their mind?'

'They hurt,' Kira said flatly. 'I guess it's like when someone dies. The people left behind have no choice. They have to move on. And they have to do it without the person they loved.'

'But I see Dene at school every day.'

'You could pretend she's a zombie,' Kira suggested, grabbing at her throat, lolling her tongue and rolling her eyes. 'She's hungry for brains. Be careful, she might eat yours!'

The bell rang. We got to our feet.

Kira nudged me. 'Check your phone.'

I'd forgotten her little experiment. I switched on and scrolled through a few posts. An ad for a bacon stacker burger popped up. *With extra cheese.*

Kira clapped her hands. 'See! What did I tell you?'

I couldn't believe it. 'Oh my god!'

'They're listening,' Kira said, twinkling her fingers at me.

The football bounced near, past my feet. I picked it up. I was going to handball it back to the year-twelve girl who was standing there waiting for it, but instead, without really thinking about it, I lined up for a goal and kicked. To my shock, it flew straight through. *Goal!*

The girl gaped at me.

Kira whooped and gave me a friendly shoulder punch. '*Wooooooooo hoooooooooooooo!* Go girl!'

And *again* the day I won the sports day race popped into my mind. Being praised, whether it came from people in real life or online, was an addictive feeling.

'That's how you get noticed!' Kira said. 'But honestly, Tully, who gives a crap about what I think, or what *anyone* thinks. It's what *you* think, Tully. It's how you feel about you. Be proud of yourself. You deserve to be.'

And in that moment I was.

I truly was.

CHAPTER TWENTY-TWO

#Obsessed

Something about me changed. I don't know the exact thing that sparked it—maybe it was that I was fed up with being angry at myself all the time. (Turns out that being down on yourself is super-tiring.) I spent less time thinking about what other people thought, or about the things they were doing, and more time on the stuff *I* was doing. I made plans. I went places. I tried new things. I didn't obsess about who witnessed me doing it—and I didn't think about Dene and what she thought.

I couldn't avoid her at school, of course. We didn't make eye contact. Sometimes she looked my way and I pretended to be looking elsewhere. The ache in my heart gradually became less and less as I learned to make myself think about other things.

When I posted online, I hardly bothered to check

the number of people who liked it. I hearted comments to be polite, mostly without reading them. I knew I was getting a lot of attention for my art but it didn't really seem to matter. What *did* matter was making it. I enjoyed it, and I was proud of myself when I strived for something different and it worked.

I photographed all of my creations—good *and* bad—and when I scrolled through my Insta homepage I didn't see it as a Show and Tell for an audience anymore, but as a catalogue of my work; a memory bank at my fingertips. I was making it work for me. It was mine (even though I technically shared it).

I followed heaps of artists and all the hashtags that had anything to do with art. My feed was packed with different styles and mediums, Australian and international, professional and emerging (Michelle explained that *emerging* meant 'budding new artists'). I followed art prizes, galleries, blogs, deceased artist tribute pages, teachers and mentors. I read posts about techniques, craftsmanship, inspirations, successes, failures. I watched time-lapse videos of art from inception to completion. I sucked up art like I was starving and it was food. I shared lots of it with Kira, too. It was nice to have someone to bounce ideas around with.

Then one day, I was midway through watching an

artist's video on creating giant murals, and Michelle's words popped into my head—that thing she'd said about people celebrating people for doing absolutely nothing.

The artists I followed were *doing* something. They were creating things of value and beauty, and they were sharing their creations so that other people experienced joy and awe and wonder when they viewed them. These people were being celebrated and admired for what they did, *not* for how they looked or some product they were touting. It felt good to tell them so too. When I made comments, I meant them.

Another thing I stopped doing was constantly thinking about Mum and Dad. Well, that wasn't *completely* true. I thought about them, for sure, but being consumed with art didn't leave me a lot of space to think about the things that hurt. Staying busy meant there was barely time to be sad. I even posted with the hashtag *#distractionismyqueen* (which was also me saying I was no longer a *#denequeen*).

But, like always, when things were going well, they took a dive. Michelle pointed out something I didn't really want to hear.

'I'm beginning to worry about you again, Tully,' she said to me one Sunday afternoon as I sat at the dining table, working on an ink and pencil picture of a kookaburra. It was turning out well. I felt a buzzy tingling inside me as I watched it come to life. 'Can you stop that for a moment and listen to me?' she asked.

I reluctantly put down the pen. 'What now?'

She hesitated like she was choosing her words carefully. 'I'm thrilled that you're exploring your passion, Tully. Truly, I am. And your enthusiasm is to be commended. And I know I was encouraging it.'

'Why do I feel a *but* coming on?'

'*And...*' she said, very deliberately, 'I think it's a far healthier pastime than some of your previous passions.'

'But?'

'But,' she said, smiling, 'it's getting a little bit obsessive. Kind of like how you were with Dene, but with art instead. Are you feeling okay, hon?'

'I'm fine,' I said through gritted teeth.

Before she'd said that, I'd felt like a high-flying balloon, gliding far above everything. It was as if she'd made herself into a sharp pin and popped me, and all the air was whooshing out and I was shrivelling up and plummeting back to earth.

'I don't want to discourage you either,' Michelle said quickly. 'I just...well...life is about balance, and things seem a bit...*unbalanced*. You know what they say about too much of a good thing?'

'No, I don't know what they say,' I said, standing up and packing up my things. I'd finish my artwork in my bedroom. I didn't have to listen to this. One of the artists I follow, a girl only a few years older than me called Zara, says to let your freak flag fly. Do your own thing. Ignore the haters. Michelle was being a hater.

'Tully...' Michelle pleaded. 'Wait.'

'This is my homework, Michelle,' I said stiffly. 'And I need to finish it. It's due tomorrow.'

'Oh,' Michelle said, sounding surprised. 'I'm sorry. Please sit down. Don't let me stop you.'

'No thanks. I'll do it in my room.' I turned to walk away.

'You can do it here,' Michelle offered.

'Why?' I said. 'So you can lecture me?'

I felt tears coming. I didn't want her to know she'd upset me. Maybe this is why my mother seemed so devoted to her art? It takes strength—real inner strength to stick to what you love in the face of people telling you that you shouldn't be doing it *or* that you're doing it wrong. Perhaps this was the trade-off? Doing what you love meant some people will respect you for it and some will hate you. You *will* lose people along the way. You can't please everyone. And I was done with being hurt by people. D.O.N.E. Not caring about what anyone thought was a far better place to be.

Trouble was Michelle had reminded me that I *did* care.

'There's something else,' Michelle said. She went to the kitchen bench, rifled through a pile of mail, extracted a yellow envelope and handed it to me. It had American stamps and it was addressed in curly black writing. 'This arrived for you on Wednesday,' she said.

I stared at it, not bothering to flip it over and read the sender information. I knew who it was from even though I hadn't seen her writing in a long, long time.

'I want you to know that whatever is in there, you can talk to me about it,' Michelle said. 'Okay?'

My tears dripped on the envelope, smudging the ink. My mouth was dry. I swallowed hard. 'You've had this since Wednesday?' I said. 'It's Sunday, Michelle. Why didn't you give it to me straightaway?'

She said nothing. It was like she didn't have an answer.

'My mum wrote to me,' I said, choking on the words, 'and you only thought to give it to me today?'

'I thought it was better to wait for the weekend,' Michelle said weakly.

I knew *that* wasn't the truth. If she had a choice,

she wouldn't have given it to me at all.

I turned away.

'I'll be here,' Michelle called out. 'Right here, Tully. I'm not going anywhere.'

I went to my room and closed the door. I chucked my art stuff on the desk and lay on my bed.

I stared at the envelope. What did my mother want? And why now? What did she have to say? Would she tell me she was never ever *ever* coming back?

I went to open it, but instead I found myself reaching for my phone. I searched for Dene's profile. I hadn't looked at it in months. I was surprised to find she'd unblocked me.

The most recent photo was of Dene holding up a breakfast-shake packet. She was wearing workout gear and standing side-on, reflected in the mirror. She looked lithe and athletic, which I knew had absolutely nothing to do with the breakfast shake; it was her body type, her build. The text read:

Brekkiegenics. Vanilla, babes. Tastes heavenly. Looks heavenly—on you. #buyit #livingmybestlife #healthyoptions #denequeens #walkwithmewalker #ncwalker #youngandfree #livingthedream

I flipped to the previous photo. This one wasn't selling anything. Dene was holding a framed photograph of her sister, Lilly, and her face was flushed like she'd been crying.

Today would've been your birthday. It never gets any easier. Missing you is like living with an enormous hole in my heart—one I can't fill, can't avoid, can only dodge and try to move around. If I fall into that hole, I won't come out. I'll be lost in it forever. What I'd give to talk to you, to hear your voice, to read a message you wrote, to see a picture you posted. But you'll never do any of those things. I can only dream. I can only imagine what might have been. *#sisterlove #neverforget #sids #givegenerously #denequeens #walkwithmewalker #ncwalker #youngandfree #livingthedream*

As I read it my heart ached. Dene might have lied online about lots of things. She might have neglected to post stuff, omitted the truth, *stretched* the truth. But this? This felt different.

I looked at the letter from my mother. Dene's words rang in my head, playing over and over.

Missing you is like living with an enormous hole in my heart—one I can't fill, can't avoid, can only dodge and try to move around

Suddenly I knew: we all do what we do in order to cope. What I did didn't necessarily look like what Dene did, but we were both just trying to get by.

What I'd give to talk to you, to hear your voice, to read a message you wrote, to see a picture you posted

Right before me on my pillow was that very thing—my mother's voice, a message she'd written. Maybe a photo. I had more than Dene would ever have.

I opened the letter.

I scanned the thin blue sheets and noticed enormous gaps between the lines of large, loopy writing. There were small sketches between some of the lines that looked like tiny landscapes—drawings of fields of flowers and brush-grass and little trees.

I willed myself to focus on the words.

My Darling Tully,

I write this from the chemo ward, hooked to an IV drip. Thank god I can do this while I sit here, otherwise I'd go mad. Television bores me. You know I hate laptops and phones.

I'm not going to tell you that I'm sorry I haven't been in touch. The truth is I'm not sorry. I'm not sorry that you and your brother don't have to see me like this. I know your father doesn't agree, but I'm being cruel to be kind. Suffering alone so that you don't have to.

The treatment is experimental and the trial pays good money. If it works—that is, if it gives me more time, I might

be able to come back to Australia and visit.

In the meantime I make art for my sanity. I admit it's harder these days. I get tired and I have to stop and rest. It's frustrating because I have all these ideas but not the energy I need to fulfil them.

My friend, Louise, tells me you are following in my footsteps. She begs me to join Instagram, but she doesn't know me! Technophobe. She has shown me some of your recent work and I must say I found myself emotional. We are one and the same, you and me. What you do is in your nature. Whether I nurtured it or not is irrelevant. It's within you.

Just as I am and always will be,
Mum

Everything inside me came crashing down.

When you hide the truth from yourself or from others, you are capable of believing the lie.

I had successfully hidden the truth of my mother's illness in my own mind. When I'd told Dene, I'd convinced myself I was doing it to gain attention. What I was *really* doing was letting the truth escape—just for a moment—and then I was jamming my head straight back in the sand and pretending it didn't exist.

But it's as real as it gets.

Mum was on the other side of the planet dying of

cancer—a gaping hole inside of me I desperately tried to avoid.

CHAPTER TWENTY-THREE

#ByYourSide

'Luke's almost ready, then we'll drive you to school,' Michelle said as I walked into the kitchen on Monday morning. 'You don't have time for breakfast, but you can have a muesli bar for the road if you like?'

'I'm taking the bus,' I said, heaving my bag onto my shoulder and walking past her.

She looked at her watch. 'You don't have time, Tully. You'll be late.'

I leaned across the bench and grabbed a banana. I wasn't hungry, but I knew that taking something would shut her up.

'I've got five minutes to get to the bus stop.' I held up my phone to show her the Metro app.

She crossed her arms and gave me an I-know-what-you're-up-to glare. 'You can't avoid me for forever,' she said. 'We need to talk. *You* need to talk.'

'It was a stupid letter,' I said. 'Inherent in that statement is the admission I received it, I acknowledge it, and it hasn't affected me. So there.'

'Good use of the word *inherent*,' Michelle said. 'But what did the letter say? Are you okay?'

'*Do I look okay?*' My explosion took even me by surprise—it seemed to come out of nowhere. I inhaled deeply and shook it off. 'Look,' I said in a more rational tone, 'just leave it, okay? Things have been perfectly fine so far. We'll just keep doing what we were doing. When something ain't broke, don't fix it.'

Luke walked in, looking like death. There were dark circles under his eyes. He obviously hadn't slept either. I assumed he'd received a letter much like mine, though when I tried to ask him about it, he wouldn't let me into his room.

'What's going down in Dramatown?' he asked. He was trying to lighten the mood, make things normal.

But things were *never* going to be normal. Not in this family.

I played along, grateful he didn't want to talk about it either. 'What's up is that I want to take the bus,' I said. 'If I get in a car with you, you'll take thirty years off my life, scaring me stupid.'

'On the upside, you'll be old and wise before you know it,' Luke quipped. He took the Nutri-Grain out of the cupboard and scoffed a handful straight from the box. 'Consider it a cheap and free way to fast-forward the clock.' He picked up the car keys and dangled them at me.

'You two have aged me at least ten years!' Michelle said. She turned to me with pleading hands. 'Tully, our conversation is on pause. Got that? We are *going* to talk about it. That's a promise.'

I headed for the door, calling, 'Maybe in another ten years!'

As I boarded the bus, my phone flashed a message.

Luke: Mum doesn't want us to care SO DON'T

Me: On it 👍

Luke: 😊

My brother was an exceptionally well-practised liar—just like me.

The heart can't lie though. The heart does what it likes, despite what your head tells it to do. And my heart hurt so much I thought it would burn up and disintegrate.

At the third stop, Kira boarded the bus. I didn't know she was taking it today; I hadn't texted her. She saw me and ran down the aisle, plopping herself down beside me.

'I don't like Mondays,' she sang, wedging her bag

into the space at her feet. 'Mondays suck.'

'*Every* school day sucks,' I said. 'Haven't you noticed?'

She gave me a solid once-over. 'Are you okay?'

When I didn't answer, she placed her hand flat against my forehead as if to check my temperature. 'Oh yeah,' she said. 'Definite case of Mondayitis. Worse than mine. We need to operate—*stat!*'

Her words made me smile, but the touch of her hand did something else—my insides crumbled and tears rolled down my cheeks. I couldn't stop them. I turned my head to the window, hoping she wouldn't see.

'Tully?' Kira whispered, taking my hand. 'What's happened?'

I laced my fingers with hers. I couldn't speak.

'Talk to me,' she pressed.

It took me a few minutes to be able to speak.

'Remember when you told me about your mum getting sick with appendicitis?'

She nodded. 'Uh-huh?'

'How did it make you feel? That she was sick, I mean.'

'How did it make me feel?' she repeated, perplexed. 'Um, I dunno. Scared, I guess. She could've died. It was a big deal when it was happening.'

'Did she tell you about what was going on with her?'

'Sort of,' Kira said, thinking about it. 'She was quite sick and it all happened very suddenly. Because of the infection, she was delirious and in and out of consciousness, and when she was admitted to hospital, we were only allowed to visit after the surgery when she was awake.' She searched my eyes. 'Why? Is there something wrong with Michelle? Wait...Is there something wrong with you? Do you have a pain in your side?'

'No, no,' I said. 'I'm fine.'

'What is it then?'

I looked around the bus, unsure of who might hear us. I didn't want anyone to know. I didn't want their stares or their pity.

'You can't tell anyone,' I said. 'Okay?'

Kira nodded. She wrapped her little finger around mine. 'Pinky promise.'

I told her—I told her the truth about my mum—that she's dying of cancer.

Kira listened, squeezing my hand hard. She put her arm around me, guiding my head down to her shoulder. 'Tully,' she breathed, kissing my forehead. 'That's so horrible. I had no idea. I'm so sorry you've been carrying that around all this time.'

I stayed there, my head against her, crying as the bus drove down the road. I didn't need to say any more or to explain further. Kira didn't want anything else from me.

Kira was a good friend. A *best* friend. She was there when I needed her.

I thought of Dene and how I'd felt when I talked to her; how she made me feel like I was the centre of the universe. I thought what we'd shared was special, but now I knew it wasn't special at all—it was special because of what *I* was prepared to give. Before Dene, I couldn't open up and I couldn't let go of the things that hurt. I didn't know how. But it's like Dene *taught* me how, and now here I was, doing a better job of it with Kira.

A couple of bus stops later, a group of girls got on, giggling loudly. They sat a few rows in front of us. I didn't notice Dene to begin with, but when I did I saw that she was completely focused on whatever the girls were laughing about; she didn't look behind her and she didn't see me.

I lifted my head from Kira's shoulder and looked out the window. Kira was still clutching my hand. She was there, by my side.

Maybe that's all you need. Someone by your side.

The girls talked loudly enough for me to catch

parts of what they were saying. Their sentences inter-weaved, a soup of words unmistakably singing to the same tune:

She's such a cow. Can you believe what she did? How hilarious was it when she overheard us saying stuff? Did you see her face? She thinks she's pretty, but she's nowhere near all that. She uses too much eyeliner. Her bum is too big. Her thighs could block a doorway! And what's that awful perfume of hers? It smells like dog biscuits. I'm gunna set up a fake account and tell her I'm in love with her. How funny would that be? I'm gunna post that picture—you know, the one of her eating cake with it smeared all over her face.

'Nice!' Kira said.

I felt bad for the girl they were ripping into. 'I wonder who they're talking about?'

Then I heard a name—*Maddy*. They were talking about Maddy.

And Dene wasn't defending her. She was joining in. If anything she was the central cog, the others revolving around her, hanging off her every word. They were saying things to please her, to get a reaction.

You know how when you're in a car and you see something by the roadside, and you turn and do a double-take, not sure of what you saw? That's how

I felt when I looked at Dene. It was like all those months ago I'd seen something and I'd got it wrong.

Dene held up her phone and got the others to crowd into the shot, yelling, '*Dene Queens!*' I watched as she took another selfie, this one with only her in the frame. I knew which one she'd post. If I cared, I'd check, but I didn't anymore.

A stupid little photo of a random moment on a bus hardly mattered.

There were bigger things to worry about.

Much bigger.

CHAPTER TWENTY-FOUR

#RealLife

Ms Brian thought my kookaburra drawing was pro-digious. She took it from me and paraded it around the room. 'You've really blossomed these past few months, Tully,' she gushed excitedly. 'It's a stunning transformation. Truly.'

Kira nudged me and whispered, 'Hardly! She just didn't notice before now.' She rolled her eyes. 'Seriously! She's acting like she's discovered the moon. Meanwhile, others'—she proudly placed her hands flat to her chest—'have already been to Tullyland and put up a flag.'

I laughed. 'You have a way of saying things.'

Kira grinned. 'I think you may have discovered the key to success.'

'I have? What's that?'

'If no one notices what you do or how good you are

at it, don't whinge about it, just keep working. Create a mountain of art so freakin' big people are like *Oh! This has been here all this time? How did I miss this? Quick everyone, come look!* And they'll act exactly like Ms Brian—swooning over you like you're a fresh new thing when really you've been here for ages and she's the last one to the party.'

'I won't forget that *you* were the first to believe in me,' I said.

Kira winked. 'I won't let you!'

My phone buzzed. I took it from my pocket and sneaked a peek.

I couldn't believe my eyes. There was a comment on my bird post from Dene.

Dene: You are so VERY talented, Tully. This is totally amazeballs. I love looking at your art. Please keep making/posting it

Kira looked worried. 'What's wrong?' she asked. 'Is it your mum?'

'No,' I said, shoving my phone back in my pocket. 'It's nothing. Don't worry about it.'

I could tell Kira didn't believe me, but I didn't know what to say. My brain felt like scrambled eggs. Dene had commented *and* been complimentary. Why? And why now?

Ms Brian handed back my artwork. 'Be proud

of your work, Tully. You are the very reason I enjoy teaching.'

Blushing, I slid the picture into my folder. 'Thank you, Ms Brian.'

'Didn't you say your mother is an artist?' Ms Brian asked.

She could've launched a grenade. The hair on my arms stood up, hot prickles coursed through me. I looked around the room, not wanting anyone to notice.

'Yes,' I said. 'She hasn't done much lately though.'

I'd hoped Ms Brian would leave it at that, but she said, 'I'd like to see her work. Does she have a website? Do you have any photos?'

'Um...sure. I'll send you a link to the gallery.' Something hot and acidic was climbing my throat. I was going to throw up. 'I'm sorry, I need the bathroom.'

'Oh yes,' Ms Brian said. 'Of course. Everything okay?'

'Yes, I'm fine.'

Kira put her hand on my arm. 'Are you sure?' she whispered.

I nodded and hurried from the room.

I went to push on the girls toilets door, but it swung open and a surprised face stared back at me.

'Tully,' Dene said.

'Hi,' I said awkwardly, before edging past her and running for a cubicle.

'Tully?' she called.

There was no time to close the door. I crouched down and hung my head over the toilet bowl. The walls were swaying, and the floor tiles floated and crisscrossed like an Escher drawing gone wrong. My insides were upside down.

I heard her behind me. 'Tully? Are you okay? Can I get you something? Water?'

'No.'

'Is it bad? Should I get a teacher?'

'No,' I insisted. 'I'll be fine. I just need a minute. Please leave me alone.'

I heard her go, but a moment later she was standing behind me again.

'I'll wait,' she said, 'to be sure. You don't sound good.'

'Suit yourself,' I sighed, frustrated and not caring anymore.

And right at that moment it struck me that I actually didn't care. Dene could stay or Dene could go. It made no difference. Once I would've given anything for her attention, for her approval, for her to be by my side, for her to care like she was caring now. Now the way I'd felt before seemed stupid.

'I've been following your posts,' Dene said, trying to make conversation. 'You have so much talent.'

'Uh-huh,' I said, my head still over the toilet. 'I saw your comment. Thanks for that.'

'A lot of people are taking notice.'

I didn't say anything.

'Does it make you happy?' she asked.

'Does *what* make me happy?'

'That people notice.'

I tore off some toilet paper, stood up and wiped my mouth. I hadn't thrown up, but my mouth felt watery-gross.

I turned to look at her. Her eyes were soft, and she fidgeted with her dress, pulling it straight, smoothing it out. She seemed nervous or something.

'I don't care about what people think, Dene,' I said. '*Doing* it makes me happy.'

She gave me a weak smile. 'Well, that's good, I guess.'

I looked over her shoulder, at the sink. 'Excuse me, I need to wash my hands.'

She jumped out of my way. 'Oh. Right. Sorry.'

I turned on the tap, pumped some soap and scrubbed. When I looked up at the mirror, Dene was directly behind me, staring at me.

'What?' I said to her reflection.

'Are you feeling better?'

I turned off the tap and wiped my hands on my jumper. 'A bit.'

'Tully...'

I turned to look at her. 'Yes?'

'You seem—' She stopped. Her voice was quiet and unsure, and it was strange to hear her sound like that. 'You seem...*different*. I'm not sure how to describe it.'

She went to say something else, but I cut her off. 'What does it matter to you?'

Her mouth hung open.

'I mean, I get it,' I said. 'You're interested now you think I might be someone.'

She stuttered, 'That's not true...'

'Isn't it? You didn't seem to care before.'

She blinked at me, looking lost.

'You know, Dene, I used to think that what you did was amazing. All your followers and all that stuff you got for free. But I'm the one *doing* something. I make things. What do you make? Actually, remind me of what is it you do?'

She looked wounded. Then her expression slowly hardened. 'Wow,' she said. 'You *still* have no idea.'

I waited.

She stood back, her hands curling into fists. 'You

think that what I do is meaningless? You think that me posing with a diet muesli bar or some new face cream is just unimportant crap.'

I shrugged. I never used to. I did now.

'That *crap* represents people's jobs,' Dene said. 'When I promote products, people buy them, money goes to those companies and the people who work for them get paid. It means they can buy a house, drive a car, have a family, have a life, eat food, pay their bills. I get paid too. My mum gets paid. Customers pay for a service and they receive it. It's called *business*, Tully. It's how the world goes round. Buy and sell.'

'It's a lie,' I said.

'Which part?' she asked.

'You lie *all* the time, Dene. You put stuff online that you don't mean and you say stuff about the products that isn't true. You act like you care when you don't care at all.'

She pulled a face. 'Oh, and you've never told a lie before?'

Ouch. She had me there.

Dene shook her head. 'You're actually super-judgmental, Tully. And for the record, just so you know, I kept our friendship private. I kept our secrets *secrets*. Would you like for me to go online and share those?'

I bit my lip, remembering our sleepovers, the private things we shared.

She stepped forward and poked a finger into my chest. 'This is real life. You and me. Standing here. Talking. Online is *online*. It's not real.'

'Uh-huh,' I said. 'Tell that to Maddy.'

Her face drained of colour.

'I heard you,' I said. 'On the bus.'

She didn't seem to know what to say.

'How do you think Maddy feels when she receives nasty messages?' I said. 'How do you think the person who had an unflattering photo posted without their permission feels? What about a kid whose mum publicly shared how he wet the bed for five years? What you say online matters, Dene. *It matters!* Think about it.'

She swallowed and said quietly, 'You mattered to me.'

'Then why were you hiding me?'

She stared at me, genuinely confused.

'You took all those photos of us and you never posted one. Not one. You hid me like you were ashamed of me.'

'*Ashamed of you?*' She pulled out her phone. 'I was protecting our privacy, Tully! I was separating business and pleasure. I was *trying* to be respectful.

Mum told me to always be mindful that not everyone lives in the public eye like I do.'

I felt a stinging in the pit of my stomach. It made sense. It made *perfect* sense. I'd got it wrong. *How did I get it so wrong?*

'But whatever!' Dene huffed. 'If it matters to you that much, let me clear that up for you right now.'

She moved in for a photo but I stopped her. 'You don't need to do that.'

'But you just said—'

'It doesn't matter. Not like it used to.' And it was true—it really didn't.

She put her phone back in her pocket. 'You said just now that I never seemed to care before.'

I nodded.

'I *did* care, Tully. I cared more about you than I've ever cared about anyone.' She looked at her shoes and added quietly, 'But I never know for sure if people like me for me, you know? I didn't know if *you* liked me for me.'

I knew what she meant—at least I did now, after the art stuff. She could've been talking about us both.

'People always want things from me,' Dene said. 'They want, want, want, and they take, take, take. I told you the first time I met you that people think I'm confident when I'm not.'

She did—I just didn't believe her.

'I might act like I don't care,' she said, 'but I do. I just don't show it—at least, not in real life.'

We stood there for a moment not saying anything.

'Dene?'

'Yeah?'

'I'm sorry. I got a lot of stuff wrong.'

A smile spread across her face. 'I did too.'

'I need some time though…' I said, backing away to leave.

She gulped and looked sad again. 'Tully?'

'It's not about you,' I said. 'Believe me when I say that. Okay?' It was true. For once, it really wasn't about Dene.

She nodded.

'I'll talk to you soon.'

'Okay,' she said. 'Promise?'

'Promise.'

CHAPTER TWENTY-FIVE

#Exhausted

I didn't even manage to get my key in the front door before Michelle swung it open and greeted me, a sauce-spattered wooden spoon clenched between her teeth, her laptop balanced in the palm of her hand.

She took the spoon from her mouth and said, 'Yep, just give me a moment,' to the screen, before holding the laptop high and doing a slow pirouette. 'Any better? What about now?'

She was chasing the wi-fi signal. She must've been in a Zoom meeting. I'd tried to tell her to buy a wi-fi extender, but she didn't listen.

She handed me the spoon. 'Quick, go stir the pasta sauce. It's going to stick.'

I dumped my bag in the hallway and headed for the kitchen. When I got there, I stopped dead in my tracks.

'*Dad?*'

He stood up and threw his arms wide. 'Button!'

I ran to him and hugged him. 'Dad! I didn't know you were coming home!'

I turned to look for Michelle as if to say she didn't tell me. She walked in, laptop down low this time, screen tipped up at her face. Whoever she was in a meeting with had a terrific view of her nostrils and chin hair.

Dad glanced Michelle's way. 'She's just finishing up. Best keep it down till she's done.'

He took the spoon from me, went to the stove and stirred the pasta sauce.

'Hang on! I'll try something else,' Michelle said to the screen. She left the room again.

'What are you doing here?' I asked Dad. I couldn't believe he was standing in front of me, three dimensional, totally real. I wanted to hug him again just to be sure.

'First of all,' he said, turning down the hotplate, 'technically, I live here. Second: work has been going well and I thought it was safe to take my foot off the pedal and enjoy some family time. Third: I love you and I miss you.'

His slicked-back hair had more grey flecks than when I'd seen him last. And he had spiky white stubble on his chin. He looked fit in his denim jeans and a football guernsey—probably from one of his clients. It made me think of Dene and what she'd said about business, about jobs and keeping people employed, the money coming in and food on the table. Here was my dad quite literally stirring our dinner—dinner he and Michelle had paid to provide.

'How was school?' Dad asked. He gnashed his teeth and braced himself as if the answer would be bad. 'Or is that a loaded question?'

I shrugged. 'School is school.'

'Right,' he said, like he understood. He stirred the sauce and didn't look at me when he asked, 'And what about that other stuff you were having trouble with? The stuff with your friends. Has it settled down?'

'I suppose,' was all I could bring myself to say. The words he didn't know I'd overheard still echoed in my mind—that I would get over it and next week there'd be a new problem.

'I hear you've had a letter from your mum,' Dad said.

I avoided answering that with, 'Where's Luke?'

'He went out,' Dad replied.

His strained face made me think something must have gone down between them before I'd arrived home; they'd had a fight. I checked my phone. There were no messages from Luke. I thought he might've tried to tell me about Dad being here. Maybe he was too angry?

'So, coming back to your mother,' Dad began.

But that's when Michelle walked in, huffing and puffing like she'd run a marathon. 'I swear I just walked the Simpson Desert trying to get this stupid thing to work,' she said, dumping the laptop on the table. 'The sound kept dropping out. I thought I was going to have to do an interpretive dance.'

'Two words,' I said. 'Wi-fi extender.'

'Three words,' Michelle corrected. 'Wireless fidelity extender. But I'll give it to you.'

Dad put down the spoon, walked over and kissed Michelle on the cheek. 'I can help you with that tomorrow if you'd like,' he said. 'We can go shopping.'

Michelle patted his arm. 'Sounds good, hon.'

I watched them cuddle. Dad was trying, and Michelle looked like she was forgiving him. Maybe some relationships aren't completely broken. Maybe some can stretch out of shape and then come back to the way they used to be.

'I've got dinner under control if you two want to catch up?' Michelle offered.

'Sure,' Dad said. 'That'd be great. Tully, why don't you come with me?' He put a hand on my shoulder and guided me to the living room.

I knew what this would be about. I didn't want to talk about Mum.

'Dad, I already told Michelle it's no big deal. I'm handling it. Honestly.' I was doing the thing I always did with my dad—making the problem small, trying not to take up space, trying to be a good girl.

Dad gestured to the couch. 'Go on. Sit. Maybe *I* want to say some things about me, hey Button? I hope you'll listen, because it's time I was honest with you.'

I sat down and grabbed a cushion, hugging it against me like it was a life raft. My heart was beating fast.

Dad sat opposite, his hands clasped, head hung low.

'I haven't handled things particularly well,' he began. 'The truth is I haven't handled them at all. What's been going on with your mum...it's pretty big. It felt bigger than me. Bigger than *all* of us. When she shut me out and wouldn't talk about her diagnosis, I didn't know what to do. I tried to talk sense into her. Believe me, I tried. But she wouldn't listen. She's headstrong, your mother. It was one of the qualities I admired and loved about her.'

It was strange to hear Dad use the word 'loved' in relation to Mum. It had been a long time since

I'd heard him say something like that—or anything like he was saying now. This is how we Sinclairs survived. We circumvented the hard stuff and kept moving. If we were a video game, we'd be Donkey Kong—jumping barrels, weaving past stuff thrown down upon us.

'I've been angry with your mum for how she's approached her illness,' Dad said, 'but I realised the other day that I've been doing the *exact* same thing. I've been hiding too. I ran away from the situation. Buried myself in work so I didn't have to think about it. Stopped seeing you and speaking to you every day so you didn't remind me of it either.'

My chest ached and I couldn't look at him. This is what I'd been avoiding, what we were *all* avoiding— the pain that demanded our attention and threatened to swallow us whole.

'I've spoken to your mum,' Dad said.

I looked at him. 'You have?'

He shook his head.

At first I thought he meant he *hadn't* spoken to her, but then I realised he was indicating he hadn't had any success changing her mind. I know how the conversation would've gone. He would've begged her to come home, to let us take care of her. He would've pleaded with her to see sense; that her approach was

241

causing us even more heartache. That just because we didn't see her go through her illness, it didn't mean we weren't suffering.

He would've said all the things.

She would've denied *all the things*.

'I can't fix her,' Dad said. 'But I can fix me.'

I choked back tears.

'I can improve how *I* handle this,' Dad continued. 'And I want you to know that I'm going to do better from now on. Michelle has been—*very* fortunately for me—good at picking up the pieces. But it's time I stepped up. It's time I admitted that I've failed you.'

I went to argue, but he held up his hand.

'You're my daughter, Tully, and you're the kid in this equation. Your peace with the world shouldn't be contingent on having to constantly forgive me and maintain the status quo.'

I didn't know what he meant. *Status quo?*

Dad smirked. 'Do a Michelle and look it up. What I'm saying is: it's time I helped to carry the load.'

'Dad?'

'Yeah?'

'Why are you saying all this now?'

He hugged himself, cupping his elbows. 'I guess because you can only run for so long before you become exhausted.' With a heavy sigh he added, 'And

I'm so bloody exhausted, Tully. You have no idea.'

I *did* have an idea—I was tired too. 'Are you staying for good?'

He nodded. 'I have to go back to Sydney and tie some stuff up, but that's the plan. I'll work remotely from here. We *do* live in the age of technology.'

'Not without a wi-fi signal we don't,' I said.

He tipped his head. 'Hence, I said I'd take Michelle shopping.'

'Hence, that wasn't a selfless act after all,' I replied.

'Careful,' Dad warned, smiling. 'Hey. Maybe I could get your mum to agree to a Zoom or something? I could ask. No promises, but I can try...'

'Maybe.' But I knew that that probably wouldn't happen.

And with that thought, my tears came flooding back. Barely able to get the words out, I squeaked, 'Is she going to die before we get to talk to her?'

Dad sat next me. He took me in his arms and held me tight. 'I don't think so. Like me, like all of us, she can only run for so long.'

CHAPTER TWENTY-SIX

#NoFilter

The next morning while we were at the table eating breakfast there was a knock at the door. Luke answered it, wearing only his boxer shorts. On the shame-o-meter, he was a solid zero.

'Tully!' he called. 'It's for you!'

Michelle looked at her phone and pulled a face. She stirred her bowl of porridge. 'It's seven-thirty. Who comes around at seven-thirty?'

Dad ruffled my hair. 'My girl is popular, eh? What can I say? It's genetics.'

I rolled my eyes at him. I got up and went to the door. Luke passed me in the hallway, pointer finger doing circles by his temple. 'Weirdo,' he said.

'Double-Weirdo,' I said back.

When I saw who was standing on the doorstep, I rubbed my eyes to make sure I wasn't seeing things.

Dene held a finger to her lips, shushing me. She bent down and picked up a rolled-up piece of white cardboard. There were others too, stacked in a small pyramid.

She held it up for me to see.

I BEHAVED REALLY BADLY

She picked up another, this one blue.

I'VE DONE SOME MEGA DOPEY THINGS

As she reached for the green one, my heart started pounding.

I MISS YOU
I'VE MISSED YOU FOR A LONG TIME
I DIDN'T KNOW HOW TO TELL YOU

She picked up the red one.

YOU ARE THE BESTEST FRIEND
I EVER HAD. *EVER*

Finally, a yellow one.

IT'S NOT XMAS, BUT MY WISH IS THAT YOU'D
COME BACK

The last one made me laugh—she'd copied the same thing I'd written on mine!

She put the cardboard down, stood there and shrugged. Her hopeful eyes seemed to say, *Watcha think?*

I wanted to ask her a million things, to *say* a million things, but what came out of my mouth was: 'Why?'

'You were right,' she said quietly. 'I'm sorry. I wasn't ready to listen.'

I looked behind me. No one had followed me out to eavesdrop. I stepped onto the porch and closed the door behind me.

Cool air stroked my skin. Out on the road, morning traffic whizzed by—cars, cyclists, dogs tugging on leads.

'I talked to Mum,' Dene said. 'I *really* talked to her—about the blogging stuff, about the Instagram posts. I told her I don't want to do it anymore.'

Her words could've been one of the cars on the road losing control, careering onto the footpath and crashing through our front gate. I gaped at her. '*You're kidding?*'

She giggled at my reaction. 'We had the argument to end all arguments. I cancelled my Instagram account and I deleted all my posts before she could stop me.'

I couldn't believe what I was hearing. 'What about your business?'

She shrugged. 'Mum will have to sort something out. That's her job—or so I've found out. Apparently that's what parents do. Did you know? They look after their kids financially, not the other way around.'

I didn't know what to say. What she'd done was so brave.

'Are you taking the bus to school?' she asked.

'Um, I'm not sure. Dad's here.'

Her face lit up. 'Really?'

'Yeah,' I said, unable to contain a smile. 'He came home yesterday. He's moving back.'

'That's fantastic, Tully!' She gave me a friendly arm punch.

It felt good that she knew what it meant to me. 'It's pretty cool,' I agreed.

'Any news on your mum?' She looked at her shoes and said quickly, 'I mean, you don't have to tell if you don't want to. I know it's been a long time since we talked. I know things might've changed. Maybe things are worse.'

'No, no. It's okay,' I said. I took an extra deep breath. 'My mum has cancer. She's having treatment. She's on a special drug trial but...but...we don't know if it will work.'

It was the truth this time. It felt good to be honest with myself.

Dene's eyes grew wide. 'You don't know it will work?' she repeated.

I nodded.

'Meaning—?'

'She could die.' There. I said it.

Dene was silent, taking it in. Eventually she said, 'Well it's good she's getting help. I hope it works for her—and for you.'

I held back tears. 'Me too.'

She stared at me, her face a picture of compassion.

'What about you?' I asked somewhat tentatively. 'Your dad and the new baby?'

'Actually, it's going good!' she said. 'I got to go to the ultrasound. They're having a girl. I'm going to have a sister. A little sister! Can you believe that?'

'Wow! That's amazing!' And I was really happy for her too. I knew exactly what that meant to her.

She kicked at the cardboard. 'Where's your recycling bin?'

'It's round the side of the house. Here, I'll show you.'

She picked up the posters and I led the way.

As I lifted the yellow bin lid and she tossed them in, she said, 'It's kind of funny, don't you think?'

'What?'

'A recycled idea ending up in the recycling bin.'

I laughed. 'I didn't think of that.'

She reached for my hand and took it in hers. 'You

won't put me in the bin will you?'

I shook my head.

'Do you think we can start over, Tully?'

'That depends,' I said. 'You're not dead, are you?'

She looked at me, confused. Then, getting it, she put two fingers to her throat to check her pulse. 'Nope. Blood's still pumping.'

I did the same. 'I'm alive and kicking too. We can try, right?'

She nodded, beaming. 'Sounds good to me.'

When Kira boarded the bus she saw me and waved, but her face dropped when she saw Dene was next to me.

I yanked out my phone and bounced her a text. I watched as she stopped midway up the aisle, reading it.

Me: TRUST ME

She looked up and gave me an almost imperceptible nod.

When Kira was standing by our seat, Dene scooted over, wedging herself against the window. I was in the middle, and there was enough room for Kira to sit on the end. Three abreast was a bit squishy, but all the seats around us were taken.

Dene leant forward and said with a friendly smile, 'Hi Kira.'

I could tell she was nervous.

Kira gave me a concerned glance, but I knew she wouldn't snub Dene. 'Hi,' she said. And then Kira being Kira, she got straight down to it. 'So are you two friends again?'

Dene looked at me.

'Yeah, we are,' I said.

Kira nodded. 'Well just so you know, Dene, if you hurt Tully again I'll have to kill you.'

I laughed.

Thankfully Dene did too. 'I'll try not to,' she said.

'I'm not kidding,' Kira warned. 'I *know* people. I could have you taken care of,' she clicked her fingers, 'Just. Like. That.'

'Noted,' Dene said, playing along. 'But I promise to get it right this time. And you never know. Maybe even *we* could be friends too?'

'Let's not get too carried away,' Kira said, but she was smirking. She looked at me. 'Hey. Has Ms Brian seen your latest piece? Did you bring it with you?'

She was talking about the picture I'd posted on Insta last night. After my talk with Dad I couldn't sleep, so instead of lying there and constantly checking and refreshing social media, I got up, went to my desk and drew. I'd done a picture of Dad and Luke. It was from a photo I'd taken of them earlier that evening—they didn't know I'd taken the pic. They were in the living room alone, talking quietly, working things out. Right when Dad put his arm around Luke and Luke had leant his head on Dad's shoulder, I'd captured the moment.

I pulled out my phone. Ms Brian had created herself an account specifically so she could follow my art. She said she couldn't believe what was out there and what she'd been missing—so much beauty, so much talent!

I searched Ms Brian's Insta handle: *@MsBcooll NSchool*. She hadn't liked my picture, but that meant she probably hadn't seen it yet. Ms Brian liked *everything* I posted.

Luke had liked it. He'd commented: Stalker

'Ms Brian hasn't seen it,' I told Kira.

'Ms Brian!' Dene whooped. 'That reminds me!'

We looked at her. 'What?' I asked.

'I have to tell her something,' Dene said. 'It's part of my get-real plan. I have a list of things I'm working through and this is one of them.'

I had no idea what she was talking about.

'The painting on display in the front foyer,' Dene said. 'The one Ms Brian thinks I did? I need to tell her the truth—I didn't do it.'

Kira's mouth opened and closed like a fish. 'Wow! That's...*wow*,' she breathed.

'*Your painting is a fake?*' I blurted.

'Don't give me that look,' Dene said, unashamed. 'I'm coming clean now and that's what counts. Mum had this art tutor guy come over and help me. He practically did the whole thing. She paid him a bucket-load and made him promise not to tell anyone.' She looked down at her lap. 'He did some of my other assignments too. And if I'm extra-extra honest, I wanted to impress you, Tully. That's why I went along with it.'

My heart tugged. 'You did?'

She nodded. 'You're so good at what you do. I wanted you to think that we had that in common.' She added sadly, 'But I'm not talented. I'm nothing like either of you.'

'Maybe you're not that great at art,' Kira said kindly, 'but I'm sure you have other talents. There's probably stuff you have yet to discover.' She thought about it. 'Michelangelo painted a cupid and he washed it in this acidic stuff to make it seem older than what it was. He sold it as valuable ancient art and he made a killing, but later they found out it wasn't old at all. He was full-on fudging it.'

All of us were capable of good and bad things. Dene was, I was, Dad, Mum, Michelle, Luke, Kira—all of us. No one is perfect—not even the revered Michelangelo.

'Some of the paintings in art galleries aren't the real deal,' I said. 'They're copies. The originals are in a vault somewhere.'

'Why would they have alarm systems and infrared cameras?' Dene asked.

I shrugged. 'Dunno. Maybe to convince you that you're looking at the real thing?'

'The *Mona Lisa* is behind bullet-proof glass,' Dene said. 'But they stopped short of making her wear a vest.'

I cracked up.

'Well, anyway,' Dene said. 'It's time to stop being fake and start being real.' She pulled out her phone and put it on selfie.

We took the cue and leaned into the frame. I went to say *Dene Queens!* but she stopped me. 'Nope! No way,' she said. 'The Queens have been dethroned. From now on, we will say...'

'*Boooooooooyeah!*' Kira randomly shouted.

It was as good as anything.

'*Boooooooooyeah!*' we yelled.

Dene snapped the shot. She uploaded it and showed us. 'My new account,' she said. 'Send me a request. It's private and I decide who gets added.'

My phone pinged. She'd tagged me and Kira. The caption said: Morning hangs with cool chicks.

Kira cringed. 'Your account name is *DeneBean*?'

Dene nodded cluelessly. 'Cute huh?'

My phone buzzed a call—Luke's number. I answered, 'Hello. Very important person doing very important things. This had better be good otherwise aforementioned VIP will terminate this interaction ASAP.'

'Hey weirdo, check your messages,' Luke said.

I looked at my texts. He'd sent me a link.

'What's that?' I asked. 'The key to your safety deposit box where you've stashed millions of dollars for your beloved sister?'

'It's the link for our Zoom meeting,' Luke said.

'Our what?'

'With Mum.'

I couldn't speak. *What did he just say?*

'Are you there?' Luke asked.

'Uh-huh,' I managed.

'She's agreed to talk to us,' he replied.

Hot prickles spread over me. I couldn't believe it!

'Gotta go! I'll tell you more later.' Luke sounded like he was dropping out. 'I'm in the car. Bluetooth isn't working properly. Everything Michelle touches turns to crap.'

'Yeah yeah, blame me!' I heard Michelle say. 'Have a good day, Tully! I love you!'

'I love you too,' I said.

I hung up and stared at my phone.

'What's up?' Kira wanted to know.

'That was Luke,' I said. 'We're going to talk to Mum tonight—at least, I think that's what he said.'

Kira took my hand, grinning like mad. 'Seriously, that's the best news, Tully!'

Dene took my other hand and squeezed it. 'Same.'

I sat there, squished between them, feeling safe and happy. 'A lot is happening, huh? Life can be a bit bonkers sometimes.'

Dene nodded. 'But this is life without a filter.'

'Hashtag *no filter*,' Kira said.

'I think I like it better that way,' I said.

And I meant it—I totally did.

#kiratullydenebffsforever #boooooooyeah

Acknowledgments

I work largely in isolation, lost inside my own head. That said, at the end of a day of hammering away at my keyboard I must emerge to join other humans. Thank you, Daryl and Dillon. You know how to bring me back to earth with a thud. You come first. Always.

To Vikki Wakefield: you read *Selfie* in its infancy, blew adequate smoke up my skirt, then promptly served me the sh*t sandwich. I love ya, my SG. I'm an emotional basket case and yet you hang around—which is somewhat of a revelation. But hey, I'm pretty funny, so there's that. Also: wine.

To whom this novel is dedicated, Andrea Altamura: I love you too. If this novel is about friendship and all its complexities, it's safe to say you define what a brilliant friend looks like. I'm a lucky gal.

To my agent, Jane Novak, I adore your honest no-BS approach and I am lifted by your belief in me.

You give me much needed comfort and you keep me rolling the dice. Thank you to my bookings agent, Becky Lucas. You're the Shaw to my Smith. Thank you, my treasured friends Katrina Germain and Kristin Weidenbach. You're always there, and that means the world.

To the team at Text Publishing: your enthusiasm has been a massive shot in the arm. Thank you for bringing this baby into the world. To my editor, Jane Pearson: you have that beautiful old-school quality of decorum and grace. You've very patiently walked me through all my fluff-ups, gently coaxing this beast from its shell, making *Selfie* truly shine. Thanks also to Eden Thomas: I appreciate you saving me from the cringe factor.

I've thanked you in the back of other books, Judy Blume, but I'll shamelessly do it again. You remain the reason I do what I do. Naming one of my protagonists Dene is a homage to *Deenie*, the book, for me, that started it all. Your words entered my veins and became embedded in my DNA, and I'll never be able to extract you, nor would I want to. Thank you.

To the readers, bloggers, booksellers, teachers and librarians: your beautiful heartfelt comments never cease to inspire me. You help me to dust myself off and get back to work. You're the fuel that keeps me going. Thanks also to LoveOzYA, SCBWI, eKIDS, the CBCA, the ASA, festival coordinators, and fellow authors and creators: belonging to this network of amazing creative empathetic souls is the cherry on top of doing what I love.

To new readers discovering my work for the first time: If *Selfie* speaks to you and you see yourself within it, please know you are *not* defined by how many likes you get on a post. You are *not* the sum of content on a social media page. You are *not* a product designed for consumption.

You are beautiful and special and uniquely you. As a famous writer, Oscar Wilde, said: *Be yourself; everyone else is already taken.*

It's perfectly okay for you to take a while to figure out who you want to be. I'm still working it out—and I wrote this book!

#Selfiebook #Ihopeyouloveit

Kids Help Line kidshelpline.com.au
1800 55 1800